To Josh Garner,

I hope you enjoy my book. Thanks for being interested.

Michael Rubin

NATIVE SOUL

BY

MICHAEL RUBCIC

NATIVE SUN
PRESS

SUMMERLAND, CALIFORNIA

ACKNOWLEDGMENTS

Thanks to my family for supporting my desire to finish this wonderful story and for providing an inside perspective on the many tribulations kids face as they grow up; and to my mother for giving me the gift of life and instilling in me a great appreciation for early California history.

Cover Photography/Design: Ad Ventures Advertising

ISBN 0-9746848-0-5

First Edition

Native Sun Press

P.O. Box 1139

Summerland, California 93067

This book is dedicated to my lovely wife Andra,
and to my children, Ariana and Luke, who have exceeded
my highest expectations and never cease to amaze me
to this very day.

∼ 1 ∼

Two shark eggs bobbed serenely in the shallow tide pool, recent castoffs from last night's storm. Frederico tried gamely to rake the casings closer with a long stick. Attached securely to the kelp, the hand sized pods held tight. Frustrated, the twelve-year-old rancho boy gave up, slumped his shoulders, and sat down dejected.

Behind him his father's warehouse occupied the largest cave of seven at Cave Landing. Used for decades as a smugglers stash place, legends persisted of buried treasures, lost gold mines, even the resting place of explorer Cabrillo's jewel encrusted sword.

Sent by his father to retrieve bales of jerky, Frederico waited by himself, abandoned by his older brothers. They'd done this before. It was one of their many torture tactics.

Beyond the first reef cave another series of deeper caverns pockmarked the cliff. The twins, Miguel and Carlos, fourteen and full of venom, were looking for Cabrillo's sword. Down below their baby brother was merely an inconvenience, or better yet, a suitable target for their teasing. They decided to let Frederico wait. First, there was treasure to find.

Frederico gazed out at the sea. Slathered across the light blue sky, white strokes of fluff crept up on the horizon. These innocuous clouds heralded the first twisted swirls of a storm front. The spikes of which would miss their part of the coast, slamming furiously to the north.

Frederico, fresh of mind, was a mamma's boy blessed with an innate wisdom and an extraordinary curiosity. The world beyond the rancho captivated him, preoccupying him with wonder, stoking the passions of a true spirit. Small of stature but big of heart, Frederico was no match physically with his older brothers.

The oldest, Juan, was twenty years old and already a man. Frederico liked him better then the others. He had always given Frederico his due respect, even allowing him to say his part when appropriate. The twins, however, were a different story. They abused Frederico relentlessly. Outwardly justifying their actions with the ridiculous notion they were doing him a favor by toughening him up. Their mean spirited ways scared and intimidated Frederico. Luckily, Frederico's intelligence reached far beyond the grasp of all his brothers. Plus, a large dose of humility and his humble nature allowed him to use his wits to his advantage, all sadly necessary to survive with the twins.

The twins, Carlos and Miguel, were similar facially, but polar opposites. At 5' 4" they were somewhat shorter then Juan but still towered over Frederico. Miguel's barrel chest and thick wrists gave him the coarse look of a thug capable of great anger. He was the bully leader of the two. Carlos, of similar height but far less stout was definitely the subservient. Mild mannered, he was easily swayed by the brutal threats of Miguel. Carlos, forced to accept his lesser role, went along begrudgingly always playing henchman for his sinister brother Miguel.

Frederico had waited a long time for his brothers to return. He finally fell asleep, dreaming about his dear sweet mother. She had left him barely a week into their family's first year on the rancho in January of 1839.

Uprooted from her family in Santa Barbara, thrust into the unfamiliar role of rancho matron, Josefa suffered a mental breakdown during the transition. Unable to deal with her ranting and raving, Frederico's father, the Captain, sent her away to rest in an eastern sanitarium. Now, it was nearing the end of October 1840, and Frederico had been miserable ever since.

"Get up cry baby!" Miguel boomed as Carlos kicked sand all over his face.

"Come on, wake up sissy!" Carlos whined, as more sand pellets jarred Frederico out of his only solace, sleep.

"I'm up. Stop. I'm getting up now!" Frederico whined in his typical nasal drawl. His brothers laughed hysterically at their younger brother.

Miguel tapped Carlos on the shoulder and gave him that head nudge that meant it was time to go.

"Bring the bales!" Miguel snarled at Frederico, who had already tied the jerky bales to his overloaded horse.

Before Frederico could mount up the twins dashed off, leaving him in quiet introspection. He sighed deeply, hurt emotionally by their cruel tactics. Without his mother around and with his father too busy with rancho business to help, Frederico faced a challenging future. Only one card remained in his favor. The steady support of Alou, his fifty-year-old native nanny. She had carried him through recent tough times and without her he almost certainly would have lost his mind by now.

Assigned to Frederico by the Captain after his wife was sent to the sanitarium, Alou's main daily responsibilities revolved solely around Frederico. The strong Native American woman had helped the boy, cheerfully pumping up his ego the best she could. To Frederico's advantage she was constantly there for him. Although Alou couldn't fill the gap left by his mother's absence, she provided friendly advice openly and lovingly.

After several hours of trudging through the wet sand Frederico could barely make out his distant brothers. They were but specks far down the long beach. With darkness falling Frederico started to get scared. Lots of bears inhabited these coastal dunes and marshy lakes. He didn't want to encounter them at night so he decided to find a new short cut. One he had never considered before.

Frederico's uncanny sense of direction told him the main trail doubled back just inland to his current point in the dunes. By his reckoning the trail was straight over the mountain sized dunes looming before him and blocking his view inland.

Frederico led his horse up the face of the first sand ridge. After several sweaty minutes of climbing, Frederico reached the top and was greeted by a vast strand of dunes standing between him and the green interior.

"Well, let's go. There's no turning back now," the boy said to his horse. For the next two hours Frederico and his horse trudged up and down countless sand dunes. It was taking much longer then he expected, almost twice as long. Miguel and Carlos were long gone, unconcerned with

Frederico's scary plight.

At the apex of the last hill Frederico looked across a lush fertile swath of green tules and tall willows. This oasis in the dunes sat near a freshwater lake. The scene was surreal. Ducks floated down from the sky above while peace reigned supreme.

After several stunned moments something caught his attention. Near the base of a small plateau by the lakeside the remains of an ancient native village lay in plain sight. Most of the old village was in ruins. Rotted willow poles of long gone tule huts jutted from the terrain, broken by nature's elements. Some kind of misfortune had destroyed the old village. All of the huts had been burned to the ground and their occupants had never returned to rebuild.

The chirping of a scrub jay caught Frederico's attention. Walking over a small brush covered sand dune the young boy stopped dead in his tracks. Evidently, not all of the huts had been destroyed. One still remained intact.

The old tule hut looked free from damage or neglect. A wave of intrigue swept over him inspiring the spirit of adventure in his soul. Frederico descended down the long sand dune to the edge of the hut and stood transfixed. Through a small hole in the side of the structure he could scarcely believe his eyes. Inside the thatched hut lay perfectly preserved artifacts from long ago. Frederico stumbled and sat down in awe.

The tule hut was remarkable. Conical in shape, the old native dwelling sat twisted by the elements near the rambling path of a creek. The hut had been built in a low area not far from the ocean waves. Nearby, a mountain of clamshells discarded by generations of natives gave the old deserted village the appearance of an ancient dump.

As a small boy Alou had told him many stories about the old villages that once flourished along the coast. His imagination ignited a fire in his heart, stoked by her supernatural tales of demons and spirits. Alou had told him of the vastly different social structures of her tribal life. Heroes of the past were heralded in her lively stories of infinite wisdom and fabled strength. The stories took different twists and turns but were always based on Alou's personal knowledge.

Frederico was well known among the native rancho servants. They appreciated his driving desire to learn more about them. He absorbed every small detail like a sponge. Recited by Alou, the storied histories left quite an impression. One centered around an ancient native settlement in the dunes and the beautiful feather blankets made there by the original inhabitants. Finely crafted examples of native craftsmanship, these large comforters had great value as warm blankets.

Frederico pushed aside the intertwined tule thatch covering the hut. Black soot from the fire pit inside stained his hands black. He tried rubbing it in the dirt but the stain remained. Frederico wondered whose house this was and how things must have been so different when the village thrived. Peering into the dim interior Frederico's heart raced when he saw the feather blanket of lore. Reaching his bony arms inside he stroked the fine feathery folds. The soft texture of the downy feathers filled him with awe. Made from the downy breast feathers of the Canadian goose, contour feathers of the snow goose, and the dark iridescent speculum feathers of the mallard, the blanket was beyond fantastic.

From where Frederico kneeled he couldn't quite reach

the blanket. An interior support branch blocked his way. The large woody fork held up a bed of bundled tules and willow supports. A large tanned deerskin was draped over one side partially obscuring another feather blanket twice as large as the first. An exceptional specimen, it clearly belonged to someone of high tribal status.

Frederico's mouth gaped open. He pulled back a large section of the tule wall, reached inside and lifted the beautiful feather comforter from its dusty perch. He was delirious with joy. Placing the first feather comforter out of harms way, Frederico crawled under the overturned couch and grabbed the other larger feather blanket. This was too good to be true. How could this particular hut have escaped the ravages of the elements? Sheltered from the prevailing ocean winds and almost completely obscured in the wooded hollow why did this tule hut stand alone? The black soot stains on Frederico's hands reminded him of the likely cause of the destruction that damaged the village. Alou had told him stories of rogue mission soldiers who torched native villages. The old crumbling structure before him took on a new meaning for Frederico. He planned to preserve the full contents of the hut. To be done in secret, in stolen moments taken from his busy schedule at the rancho. Lost treasures to comfort him in bad times, and to preserve for the next generation of rancho dwellers.

In the dimming light of sunset Frederico took a quick inventory of the contents of the dwelling, however the approaching darkness prevented him from seeing everything. He decided the feather blankets were a good haul for now. Gathering the feathery relics in his arms, Frederico wrapped them carefully in the deerskin. They were supple and rolled easily. He slung the roll over his shoulder, mounted his horse and left quickly on the darkened trail.

Not too far beyond the old hut Frederico felt a creepy feeling flow down his spine. It pierced the chilling darkness and enveloped him in its mesmerizing grip. Somebody or something stared at him from beyond his view. Frederico dared not turn around for fear of seeing angry ghosts. They must be upset with him for plundering the old village site.

Frederico rode on faster then ever. He tried plugging his ears so as not to hear the imagined cries of long dead spirits. The long low moaning noises in his head finally stopped and were replaced by the rhythmic clomping of hooves.

To Frederico's dismay the prickly feeling still hung in the air, frazzling Frederico's nerves. Stopping to catch his suddenly short breath he gathered all his courage and turned to look behind him. A strange orange glow rose from the distant village. It flickered randomly, throwing long sinister shadows across the dunescape. The glow paralyzed Frederico. The powerful spirits of deceased shamans? Alou had said they conquered death and lived forever. Some were said to take the form of glowing balls of gas and these hovering spheres haunted the old village sites. Frederico looked deep into the twilight and saw only a faint, flickering orange glow. Suddenly, the terror of his recollection squeezed his guts shaking him to the core. An old native legend said that to look upon the lights was bad spiritually. It could result in the death of the viewer. A great deal of uncertainty followed by his initial fright left him unsettled. Home was still many miles away and he needed to hurry if he wanted to beat nightfall.

Peering through weathered eyelids an old, forgotten man tended to his small fire inside the old tule hut. He was trembling with the realization that his home had finally been discovered. After nearly forty years of hiding in the brush, the sixty six year old native was unsettled. A stranger, a small boy from the rancho, had found him by chance, forever changing his life.

In the past, small bands of mission soldiers and, more recently, the curious young men of the ranchos, pushed very close but never within direct view of his hut. Ultimately, the old native sadly decided, life, as he knew it, was over. Sooner or later the soldiers would come and make him their slave. He had hoped he died before this happened.

The discovery of his house forced him to grasp the life changes before him. His wild spirit would ultimately be the last to grace his tribal countryside and this made him very sad.

Frederico rode like the wind along the dark trail, his mind racing with the alarming memory of the flickering lights. What were those lights? Could it have been the light from a campfire splashing the surrounding dunes? This was the only rational explanation Frederico could think of. Perhaps that was what he had seen. Clearly someone was still living in the dune village. Another larger question loomed in Frederico's curious mind. Who was he and why was he avoiding contact?

Up ahead the trail widened and the familiar sights and sounds of the family's rancho beckoned him. Frederico reached down and patted the roll of relics, hoping to hide them before his discovery by the twins. He knew of a hollow depression in an oak tree that would be a perfect place to put them. Frederico rode over to the tree, leaned over and placed the bundle deep in the hollow. Very carefully he pushed some dead leaves over the top. After a brief glance around, satisfied his secret was safe, Frederico returned to the house.

In the shadow of the doorway Alou, concerned with Frederico's whereabouts, was waiting. She had witnessed the boy stashing the artifacts in the tree and wanted an explanation. The boy put his horse in the corrals and walked to the house consumed with the mysterious lights in the dunes and who or what was responsible for them.

No longer impacted by the terror of the night Frederico began to strongly suspect he had seen the lights of someone's fire. Perhaps the man had seen him stealing the feather blankets. They probably belonged to him.

Frederico felt sick about stealing someone's prized feather blankets. His shortcut had started out innocently enough but somewhere along the way Frederico knew he had crossed the line. Hanging his head in shame Frederico felt the shame in his heart as his walk to the house slowed to a crawl.

Alou stepped out from behind the door, her furrowed brow full of concern.

"Frederico, where have you been? The twins said you left them and when they tried to find you, you had vanished. Where did you go?" Alou asked firmly.

Frederico's stomach did several flip-flops. There was no way he could tell a lie to Alou

"Alou, I have a terrible confession to make. On the way home from Cave Landing the twins ditched me, abandoning me on the trail. When I tried to find a short cut home I stumbled across an old native village tule hut that was undamaged. I broke in without thinking. Inside were two feather blankets. The excitement of the discovery blinded me with greed and I took them. Against all I've been taught, I stole them even though I knew these feather blankets belonged to someone else. I'm so sorry Alou. Please help me take them back tomorrow. I can't live with myself until this is done."

Alou looked more surprised then angry. Frederico had discovered her family secret in the dunes.

"Frederico, I'm glad you've had a change of heart. Of course I'll help you. We better repair the damage to the hut too. Tomorrow, we must return things to the way they were," Alou confided seriously.

Inside her heart, however, she knew this could never be. Frederico had opened up a Pandora's box and nothing could ever close it again. Alou's story of faith and perseverance would soon be revealed.

≋ 2 ≋

The next morning Alou and Frederico set out for the tule hut. Under her wide brimmed hat Alou's serious expression hinted at the importance of their journey. Her heavy jowls, darkened by years of summer sun, framed her full round face. Set deep in her brow, Alou's sparkling eyes revealed an inner glow that melted away hurts of the heart.

Deep in thought the proud native woman sought to right Frederico's wrong. The rancho boy, in his naturally curious manner, had ransacked an old native hut. Taken without intended malice, two fine feathers blanket, symbols of lost native ways, had to be returned. Alou realized this discovery would result in the revelation of the deep secret she had kept silent for years.

Frederico's bean shaped head wobbled with each step of his horse. He felt secure with Alou, his native nanny. The understanding and compassion that flowed between their souls had become his lifeline. His own mother, away in a sanitarium, was absent. Alou had stepped forward and offered to help. Fluent in her native tongue and Spanish the smart woman recognized Frederico's dire need to be nurtured. In time their love for one another became very powerful.

Sitting together on Frederico's horse, the boy in front and Alou behind, they thrived on each other's presence. Constantly nourishing a friendship remarkably complex and fulfilling.

Far ahead near the coastal dunes shifting hues of orange and purple painted the landscape as a late fall fog blanketed the chilly waters of the Pacific.

Frederico was trying to decipher his feelings of shame for his transgressions of the day before. The specter of the unknown befuddled him. If someone did live in the tule hut who was he? The thought troubled him. Perhaps a greater understanding of native ways would lead to the right answer. Naturally he turned to Alou.

"Alou, you once told me of the native spirits that resided on this rancho. You mentioned that the local natives believed there were three different worlds. What did you mean by that?" He asked.

Alou raised her eyebrows with surprise. She had told him that story one night while tucking him in bed and never expected him to remember all the details.

"Frederico, you are a curious boy. I like that. The three worlds you ask about are central to our native beliefs. We believe there are three worlds in our universe. The earth is the center of these worlds and the biggest. Hovering below us is another world that is far more sinister and dangerous. Above us floats the third world. All three of these worlds are connected in strange ways. Here on earth, in the middle world, we live surrounded by oceans leftover from the great flood. After that early catastrophe the first people who lived here were transformed into animal and plant spirits. They are the spirit forces I have told you about."

Frederico was still not satisfied.

"Tell me about those other worlds, the lower and upper ones."

Alou laughed and said,

"So many questions little boy. Come on. Let's ride faster. We have important work to do."

Frederico protested briefly then settled quietly into pace on his beautiful Arabian horse. They traveled a short distance before Alou, who could not stay silent any longer, continued her description of the three worlds.

"The lower world is a bad place. Full of mutated beings likely to cause suffering, pain, and bad luck. Sometimes in the middle of the night they would come up from their world. Disguised as humans, they were free to roam this earth and were responsible for many of our problems. They were not like the sky people of the upper world," Alou said.

Frederico shuddered. He hoped those ghostly lights were not malevolent creatures from below. Their supernatural forces frightened him.

Alou was grateful for Frederico's attentive nature. No one had ever been quite so interested in her culture.

"In the upper world the gods of the moon and sun hold court over a grand entourage of sky people. These powerful beings have some human attributes but are far superior to us mere mortals. They created man.

The upper world is held aloft on the wings of a giant eagle. This great, powerful bird flaps his wings to push the skies forward in the natural celestial cycle," Alou explained animatedly.

She stopped to see if Frederico was listening. His eyes were big, obviously impressed by her story. Encouraged, Alou continued,

"My father once told me that as Shaman, he possessed the knowledge to travel beyond this world into the other two. To attempt such a journey my father needed many skills, powerful spirit helpers, and sacred effigies. He never revealed to me what he had seen in the other worlds. Certain subjects were sacred to my father and his trips into the supernatural worlds were some of them," she noted.

The boy looked straight into Alou's soft brown eyes. His growing respect for Alou and her heritage beamed forth in awesome splendor. Satisfied with her description Frederico thanked her graciously.

"You are a wonderful teacher Alou. My fondest dream is to learn all that I can about your people and the special way they lived," Frederico said happily.

Alou appreciated the pure glow of innocence within the boy. Unlike the others at the rancho Frederico sincerely cared about her and the native servants. She was not concerned with the boy's ethnic heritage. Only that Frederico's open and caring heart made him a natural student of their vanishing culture.

The trail snaked under the horse. Long stretches of which were worn smooth by repeated use. One of the rolled tule mats Alou carried became untied and fell to the ground. Frederico stopped his horse and scrambled down to pick it up. He was uncertain why she had brought the mats.

"What are these for?" He asked.

"Here, give it to me," Alou said. She pulled some cords out of a leather bag. Four strands of cleaned, twisted fiber

15

spliced together to make a piece of cord nearly three feet in length. Rolled into a small coil and tied tight, the cord appeared extremely durable.

Several coiled cords, each one a different length and ply, sat loosely in the bag. Most were two-ply strings but three of them were three-ply fibers braided together to form a thick rope. Unsure of the damage to the tule hut Alou thought it prudent to bring a wide assortment of cords to handle the widest range of repairs.

Frederico saw the neatly coiled cords in her bag and said,

"Those cords are really tight. They remind me of the leather reatas my brother Juan braids in his free time. How do you get them so perfect?" He asked.

Alou highly regarded the boy's curious nature. It identified him as someone with superior intelligence and she was eager to challenge him.

"When I was a small girl my mother taught me how to make strings and cords. We used them in every part of our lives. These cords held our world together. To insure durability we learned to make them strong and pliable. We used a plant called tok that looked like the willow. We only used the long new stalks with the reddish skin.

We pulled the plant up and dried the long stalks for eight days, then hit them with a stick to soften them. The long fibers were cleaned and processed. Usually our whole family participated," Alou explained.

"But Alou, how do you make cords from plant fibers?" Frederico asked, still unsure of the methods.

Alou tried showing him her techniques by using hand motions to mimic her methods.

"One of us would scrape off the red skin then split

16

the stalk lengthwise nearly to the end. The intact stalk was used as a handle. Next, we removed the center of the stalk, brushing any excess pith from the leftover fibers. It was best if you used good clean strands for strong strings.

When we needed to make a cord, I would take two bunches of fibers and with a rolling motion on my thigh, twist the two fibers together. The resulting string was wrapped on a stick as more and more of the fibers were spliced together.

"Do you understand?" She continued merrily.

"It was easy. Someday, when we have more time, I'll show you how." Alou said, happy to be of service to the rancho boy.

"So, you are going to use the cords to tie the hole closed, right? I understand now. Those rolled up tule mats are the patches, true?" Frederico observed.

Mottled brown and yellow, the tule mats were remarkably trim and tatter free. Rectangular in shape the four-foot by eight-foot mats were normally used by Alou as a bed liner and pillow. Frederico noticed before how she always sat on one when she rested. The long tules ran lengthwise and on one side looked as though Alou had beaten the fibers, softening them. All along the edge, braided tules had been tied with fiber cords.

"Did you make those mats?" Frederico asked, seeking to soak in more knowledge.

"Yes Frederico, I keep several rolled up in my sleeping quarters. I could never get used to the newcomer's pillows. They were too soft. In case I ever needed to make a new one I would go and gather round tules, not the flat cattail tules, and lay them next to each other on the ground. Using a bone needle and fiber cords I interweaved the twine through and around each stalk, drawing them together from time to time to make them tight. I did this in rows about a foot apart," Alou instructed, proud of her skill in making tule mats.

Frederico singled her out for praise.

"Alou, everything you do you do with such style. I'm in awe. When I grow up I hope I can do these things too," Frederico chirped, happy as a lark.

Alou smiled and rode on. Her young charge Frederico had not mentioned his suspicions about the mystery man still living in the old village. In her concerned mind she rolled around the identity of the mystery man known to her and her alone.

Alou and the boy continued for a while on horseback before branching off the trail and scooting under some low sweeping willows. Several hundred yards away the canopy of trees opened up revealing the deserted village against a backdrop of high sandy dunes. Cleverly concealed by branches the damaged tule hut stood erect. Framing the doorway, a six foot tall jawbone of a gray whale provided perfect structural support for the entry way. Bleached pale white by the sun, it must have taken hours for several strong men to carry it back to the village. In front of the door a large rectangular tule mat acted as a wind buffer. Inside, past a small vestibule, another tule mat served a similar function.

This tule hut looked small in comparison to the others that once filled the village in an orderly fashion. Slightly less then fifteen feet tall, the tule covered structure had a dome shape with an open ventilation hole near the top to let smoke out and light in. The arched willow framework was lashed together with a substantial amount of tule cordage. Frederico had ripped apart one small spot near the back of the hut to get inside. Handfuls of torn tule thatch and broken cordage lay heaped at the foot of the structure.

"Look, there's the spot I ripped open to get to the feather blankets. I'm afraid I did more damage then I remembered. I feel so stupid for doing this. Do you think we can fix it?" He asked Alou.

"Of course," she said with confidence,

"These native homes were built in a way to ease future repairs. A large numbers of willow poles make up the frame and provide many tie points. See these poles, we can lash my mats there."

Alou pointed to a large vertical pole and two thinner horizontal poles. She unrolled her mats and fingered several different coiled cords trying to gauge the strength. Alou picked two coils of the same size and prepared the hole by cleaning away enough tule to get a firm anchor. Weathered from the ages the family-sized hut should have been torn down and rebuilt long ago.

"Is this the way they always looked?" Frederico probed.

"No, originally this hut looked much better. It began as a perfect circle etched in the dirt. Stout poles of willow, some close to twenty feet long were put in deep holes, heavy end down. The tops overlapped and were tied with strong braided ropes. More willow poles were used to form the horizontal framework. Over this frame tule stalks were layered in an overlapping manner. First, with the stalk tip up then down on the outside layers to help shed water. Around the whole hut dirt was piled up to seal the bottom. Look, Frederico, see how the door is facing east. This was to take advantage of the morning sun. They would open the tule mat flaps to let in early heat."

Frederico kept listening, intrigued with the details. By the end of the lesson she had finished her repairs. Only one of her mats was needed to cover the hole. The overlapping tule mat formed an excellent patch against the elements.

"There, I'm done Frederico. Go inside and put those blankets back exactly where you found them. Hurry, I don't want to deal with angry spirits. For your sake don't stay inside for long. We must be leaving soon," she said.

Frederico stepped inside the tule hut and gasped in wonder. All around him native tools, clothes, and furniture remained in pristine condition. Someone did live there. That much was certain. The feeling of being in someone's house was too uncomfortable to bear so Frederico placed the blankets on a long wooden bench and scrambled out. Alou was already on her horse and looked kind of nervous.

"Hurry," she insisted. "We must go!"

They left quickly.

Emerging unseen from the edge of the thick brush a native man watched as the dust cloud disappeared over the willow thicket. The solitary man smiled softly. Yesterday, he had witnessed the boy taking his prized feather blankets and this had disturbed him greatly. He was glad the boy had a change of heart. The old native's clear eyes sparkled as he pondered the altruistic pair. The boy was obviously a newcomer but he did have his heart in the right place.

The woman with Frederico was well known to the native. Alou was his trusted and caring daughter. Unfortunately, the curiosity of the boy had been piqued. The native knew this would draw the boy back. A somber mood draped over the lonely native. After decades of freedom his presence had finally been felt. Perhaps if he stayed out of sight the boy would lose interest and forget about him. He laughed silently to himself because he knew that was unlikely.

20

≋ 3 ≋

Alou and Frederico arrived back at the rancho before noon. The boy noticed an unusual amount of activity in the courtyard and asked,

"What's going on Juan?"

"Oh, hey Frederico, Father was looking for you this morning. He has some good news for you," Juan told him.

Frederico answered excitedly,

"Where is he? Any news is good news to me."

"The last time I saw him he was getting ready over by the stables," Juan said.

"Getting ready for what?" The boy prodded.

"I'll let him tell you," Juan said, smiling at the first sign of excitement he'd seen in his little brother in months.

Frederico sprinted over to the barn. His father was inspecting several saddles and filling big saddlebags with provisions and supplies.

"Hi Father. Juan said you were looking for me. He said you had a surprise for me!" Frederico said with gusto.

The Captain barely acknowledged his youngest son, choosing instead to grunt,

"Help me with these saddles. Quit being such a pain in the rear end. Yea, I have a surprise for you. I've noticed you moping around lately and I thought you might like to go to Santa Barbara for a few days with me and my men. I have business to tend to and your mother's family hasn't seen you in almost two years. Do you want to go with us?" The Captain asked impatiently.

Frederico was slightly uncomfortable with the way his father had asked him, but the trip back to Santa Barbara was something he had dreamed of for a long time. He missed Santa Barbara and all the friends and fun it represented.

"Yes Father, I would love to go with you. Thank you so much for including me in your plans. When are we leaving?" Frederico inquired excitedly.

"We're leaving tomorrow morning early and you better be ready," the Captain warned.

It was not the Captain's idea to invite Frederico. That suggestion came from Juan who worried about his little brother. He knew his father, the Captain, could be quite distant at times, especially with Frederico. With all the work to be done on the rancho he never seemed to have enough time to spend with his youngest son. Juan hoped the two of them could be together for a short time. He knew his father needed to improve his relationship and the trip to Santa Barbara would give his father the opportunity to see just how special Frederico had become.

The next morning, before the sun came up, the whole group set out on horseback for Santa Barbara. Frederico wanted to ride up front with his father but was told to stay back. The Captain wanted to discuss the ongoing cattle operation with his foremen and didn't have the time or the desire to communicate with his son.

This uneasy situation did not quell the spirits of the excited boy. No sir, no matter what the circumstances were, Frederico was going home to revisit his wonderful childhood memories.

During the next two days the group ventured to Santa Barbara without incident. Frederico was rebuffed three more times in his attempts to pal around with his father. These jabs of indifference hurt Frederico's heart but he was non-deterred. The only thing on his mind was getting to Santa Barbara to see his old friends, especially his best friend Thad. Frederico stayed confident things would be the same as before and the anticipation kept him wound as tight as a ball. They arrived late on a warm sunny afternoon.

With the beautiful blue sea and rocky ridges as a backdrop, Frederico was reminded once again of the astonishing beauty of Santa Barbara. The air somehow felt softer and the sunshine warmer then back at the rancho.

The last time the Captain traveled to the pueblo of Santa Barbara the traditional social power structure was still in place. Most of the Captain's friends were direct descendants of the early mission soldiers and their wives. Their culture was familiar to him. Already comfortable with his native English language the Captain had become fluent in Spanish, the dominant language of the region. This made it easy for him to assimilate into their society. He had gained their trust and respect through hard work and attention to details. A reputation earned from many years of honest dealings.

Much to the Captain's dismay, familiar faces had been replaced by newcomers. Americans were very common in town now, drawn to the area by reports of bountiful lands and temperate climate.

Sore from the long ride the Captain, Frederico and the rest of the group sought rest in the shade of the old presidio wall. In earlier visits, the Captain and his large family had stayed at the home of his in-laws. That was before the Captain sent his wife away to rest in a sanitarium over the objections of her family. Bad feelings still lingered so he decided to stay the first night with an old friend. Several lived in the presidio and he was sure one would welcome him and his rancho group.

By chance, Hildago, the very friend the Captain sought out, rode by on his horse as they rested in the shade. The Captain saw him and greeted him enthusiastically.

"Hildago, you old salty dog! How have you been? How many years has it been? Two?" asked the Captain.

Hildago was very happy to see his old friend but appeared unusually subdued.

"Captain, it's nice to see you again but let me be the first to tell you that things are not well here. Big changes have left a lot of the old timers destitute. They don't have anyone to help them. In the old days, during bad times we always looked out for each other. We did it for the common good of the pueblo. Ever since the Americans came our ways of doing business have collapsed. The newcomers demand immediate payment on receipt of goods and services. They won't allow us to pay on credit. At first they had a hard time competing. Now, with bags full of gold, they have driven most of the old merchants away by ruining them with their low prices and endless supplies. Yes, my old friend, the pueblo has changed since you've been away," Hildago sadly declared.

"But Hildago, how did the newcomers get away with it? Didn't anyone resent their takeover?" The Captain asked, baffled at the ease in which the Americans had taken control.

"Yes, a few angry men confronted them but our threats of injury and death fell on deaf ears. Finally, we all gave up and accepted them. The new people from Mexico and Spain were easier to work with but the people from the American east coast and France frustrate me," Hildago related as he sighed in disgust over the whole mess.

The Captain was puzzled. When he left the pueblo to settle on his Mexican land grant rancho to the north, the new economy was prospering. He had every reason to believe it would continue. After a few minutes of contemplation he returned to the business at hand.

"Hildago, can we stay with you at the Presidio for a few days while we finish up our business?" The Captain asked.

"Sure, you're welcome anytime," Hildago responded, adding,

"Come, let's go now and get settled. We're having a delicious beef stew tonight and one of the cooks has made some tasty delights for dessert. Afterwards, we can reminisce about how things used to be."

Frederico was disappointed they weren't staying at his aunt's house. Thad lived next door to her and Frederico hoped he could play with him today. The presidio was on the other side of town and there was no telling when they might get back over there.

The Captain, Frederico, and their rag tag group of rancho foremen followed Hildago over to the Presidio and settled in for the night. Frederico kept hoping he would see a familiar face on the way but was disappointed. Many different people from all parts of the world inhabited Santa Barbara now. Frederico was disturbed to find so little left of his past life.

The Captain needed to stop by his old store, one of many business ventures he once dabbled in. In the good old days the Captain's store did a large amount of business with the mission and the presidio. The missions supplied him with woolen cloth, hats, wine, brandy, hides and tallow. His trading post grew, providing income for other ventures.

Frederico waited outside while his father conducted business. A few minutes later he emerged.

"Father, can we stop by Grandpa's house? I want to see if any of my cousins are home," Frederico requested.

His father ignored him at first.

"Father, can we stop and see my cousins?" The boy whined once more.

"No!" The Captain snapped. Business had been bad recently at the store and the man who bought it could not pay him the rest of the money he owed. This disturbed him. It was worse then Hildago had said. The newcomers were creating havoc with the established shops. No one seemed to have an answer.

The Captain himself had once been a newcomer. He originally opened his store in 1826, after a very successful stint as a merchant sea captain. He also obtained a hunting license for otters from the Mexican government and sublet it out for a percentage of the take.

The Captain met the daughter of Don Carrillo, married her, and instantly became a member of high society. He later became Captain of the port, which required him to collect port fees, duties, and compile shipping records. The residents of Santa Barbara even elected him mayor of the pueblo one year.

It wasn't until several years later that the Captain was

awarded his land grant. Unfortunately for Frederico this meant moving and severing ties to the town where he was born and raised.

Frederico's excitement was gone. In its place disappointment caused his shoulders to sag and made him unusually quiet and sullen. Nothing had gone according to the boy's hopes and dreams. Despair, instead, had raised its ugly head.

The rancho group took up residence in one of the presidio buildings and diligently took care of business. Frederico's father left early each day and didn't come back until late in the afternoon. The few soldiers and aids left behind were strangers and did not attempt to befriend him. Once again Frederico felt isolated and overwhelmingly depressed. Things in Santa Barbara were twice as bad as the rancho. He could never have imagined this.

One last hope remained, the opportunity to meet with his best friend Thad. He would understand Frederico's heavy despair. Surely Thad would help cheer him up.

Just before Frederico fell asleep his father came in and talked to him for a minute.

"Frederico, are you awake? My business in Santa Barbara will be done tomorrow. Afterwards, I was thinking about going to Grandpa's house for a visit. I'm sorry I haven't been around much. With all the work to do I haven't had the time. You understand, right?" The weary Captain asked.

The good news did wonders for Frederico. Maybe his trip would turn out okay after all.

"Father, I understand why you can't always be there for me. Work first, play second as you always say. I'm just sorely disappointed about how things have changed here in

Santa Barbara. We used to know everybody in town. Not anymore. This makes me uncomfortable. Do you think Thad will still be the same?" Frederico wondered.

"Don't worry. Some things never change. I'm sure he will be thrilled to see you," his father reassured him. The Captain bent down and gave his youngest son a kiss good night. A tender gesture too often delayed. Frederico appreciated the few minutes his father spent with him. If only he did that more often.

"Good night Father," Frederico called to his dad as he shut the door behind him. Frederico felt cold and alone and for a few brief moments allowed his mind to dwell on the pain of missing his mother. Being in Santa Barbara left him vulnerable to old memories and one of his saddest was the day his disturbed mother was secured to a carreta and carted away from the rancho. The trauma of that chaotic scene and the cries and shrieks of his dear mother had devastated the whole family. No one had questioned the Captain's directive to send his mother away and Frederico was starting to wonder if it had really been necessary. Soon sleep overwhelmed Frederico and the tired boy drifted off into dreamland.

≈ 4 ≈

Around noon the next day, the Captain and the rancho men finished their business and rode with Frederico over to the Carrillo house for a social visit with his in-laws. Frederico, greeted warmly by his grandparents, was thrilled. They all but ignored the Captain.

"Where are my cousins?" The boy asked.

Grandma Carrillo told him,

"I think they're playing next door with Thad."

His boyish enthusiasm revived, Frederico raced over to see them. In the courtyard of Thad's large house about a dozen kids played hide and seek. Thad was there along with three of Frederico's cousins and seven other new kids he had never met before.

"Thad, it's me, Frederico!" The young boy called out. The kids stopped their game and walked over to where Frederico was standing with a big smile on his face.

"Hi Frederico. How are you doing?" One of his cousins asked.

"Yea, how are you doing," Thad chimed in sarcastically, adding,

"I didn't think I'd ever see you again."

Frederico wanted to pour out his heart to Thad but hesitated. Most of the boys who were playing with him were strangers. He sensed feelings of hostilities among them.

Before he could answer, Thad, once his best friend, started to get nasty and arrogant.

"This is the kid I was telling you about who lives out in the boonies with the natives. He's the digger lover!" Thad sneered.

"Thad, why do you say such things? Our rancho needs natives to work for us. We couldn't survive without them. Besides, what do you really know about them? They're good people and work very hard," Frederico replied, shocked at Thad's insensitivity.

"Digger lover, digger lover," some of the new boys started to chant.

Frederico was horrified.

"Please Thad, make them stop," he begged, reduced to a state of tears.

Thad joined in with the other boys, teasing him and calling him names. Whatever friendship they once had was now history.

Frederico was speechless. Tears welled up in his eyes and spilled down his cheeks.

"Hey crybaby, crybaby. Look, the digger lover is a crybaby. Why don't you go home to your native diggers? We don't want your kind around here!" Thad goaded.

The humiliating pain and frustration Frederico felt in his heart came flooding out. Sobbing uncontrollably, Frederico ran from Thad's courtyard into the road. He felt lost, truly alone in this hard, cruel world. For the longest time he sat with his face buried in his hands. Every tear that fell made him even more withdrawn. It was obvious Frederico had no friends left in Santa Barbara. The young rancho boy just wanted to get the heck out of there and the sooner the better.

Two hours later Frederico's father and the rancho men left the Carrillo house and gathered their provisions. An enormous amount of work remained to be done at the rancho to insure the success of the Captain's hide and tallow business. He needed to get home. Everything else was secondary.

The group journeyed back to the rancho. Frederico's feelings had been crushed but, surprisingly, one thing kept popping into the boy's mind, an obsessive fascination about all things native.

Frederico arrived home under the sad impression that his life wasn't worth living. Alou was waiting for him. She missed her little guy. That night she went to his room and started to comb his hair.

The short comb of wood sported finely carves spines. Plainly adorned, it served servant and son alike. Alou stroked Frederico's thin black locks slowly, without pulling or jerking. The stroking motion had a soothing effect on the boy. With all his assigned chores he rarely had time to relax. Frederico settled into a comfortable position and became quite chatty. Alou's relationship and close bond with Frederico was reinforced by their conversations.

"I hope I never have to go to Santa Barbara again. Thad, that boy I told you about, was horrible. He called me names and teased me. He even called your people names. Diggers! What did they mean? My fists wanted to smash him in the mouth but I couldn't. All I could do was stand trembling, crying, acting just like they said I was, a crybaby. Alou, my heart feels so much pain. Thad would never have said those things before. Those newcomers must have influenced him. The whole time I was in Santa Barbara I saw a virtual parade of new faces and languages. Their ways are so different from ours. They have so much hatred. I wanted to welcome them into my heart but they wouldn't return my gesture. Tell me Alou, was it the same for you?"

"Yes," Alou said softly,

"Our people were affected greatly. My grandmother told me the legend of the first newcomers. I was like you, always eager to learn. She told me countless stories of our people. My life was enriched by these legends and I'd like to share some of them with you," she declared.

"By all means Alou. I want to know all about your world and the way it used to be," Frederico said with conviction.

Alou was so proud of Frederico. Childless, he was the closest thing to a son she had. At times she felt as though their spirits were connected and that they had known each other before in another life.

"My grandmother told me that in the year 1769, during the last part of the summer, an expedition led by a man named Portola camped near our village by the lake. Our people had never seen such a collection of strange beasts and equipment. Portola had 65 men and 180 animals with him. They made a line over one thousand yards long as they marched. However, they were not coming in peace and our chief disregarded the warnings. He went to their camp and welcomed them. The newcomers did not understand him and briefly detained him. After his release they followed him to our village and caused trouble there. Some of the village women were down by the

32

shore of the lake bathing when they were surprised by a group of six drunken soldiers. Several village women were assaulted. Their screams alerted some brave native men who went to their rescue. Six of our men were badly injured trying to drive the soldiers away. The women were shaken but lived to tell about it. The messengers were right. They hadn't come in peace. Luckily, Portola broke camp the next day and rode north into the tribal territories of our neighbors. Frederico, our people learned first hand about the problems with the newcomers."

Frederico was upset. Alou's voice trembled with pain decades old. His compassionate nature made him feel very sad for her.

"I'm sorry Alou. I didn't know it was such a terrible ordeal for your people. Did they ever come back?" Frederico wondered glumly, saddened by her emotional state.

"We were warned the next spring about the same group but they must've taken a different route because we never saw them," Alou confided.

"Five years later another expedition led by a man named Anza came through with about thirty five men. All the villagers hid in the tules, including my father, Paha, who was only an infant at the time. The strangers passed through quickly and were given a wide berth by all the tribes. The few natives who encountered the expedition on the trail were treated fairly in return for information about our main trails. They were given trade beads and tobacco. The next year Anza was back and this time he brought vast numbers of people, over two hundred, plus horses, mules, cattle, and something else. They brought word of their religion. After that our village was spared contact with newcomers for nearly twenty-five years. When they did come back they changed our native ways forever. The new men established missions and presidios and before you knew it our people were no more," Alou cried. She closed her eyes and sobbed softly.

Frederico felt so bad for her he cried too. The two of them together, the pain of change unleashed.

"Hey Frederico, we need you out here. What are you doing crybaby!" Miguel pricked. He had heard of Frederico's crying fit in Santa Barbara. Miguel picked up on it right away and was prepared to use it at will to humiliate his sensitive brother.

"Crybaby, crybaby! What a baby!" Miguel teased. Frederico and Alou whimpered softly, holding each other tight, unwilling to listen to Miguel's hurtful rips.

Miffed at his inability to get a rise out of Frederico, Miguel finally left the room.

"We'll see you later," Miguel scornfully reminded his baby brother. He was right. Ten minutes later Frederico wiped his tears and steadied his nerves for yet another painful day on the rancho.

Alou gave Frederico one last squeeze, then composed herself and left to do her daily duties. Frederico went downstairs to face his vile older brothers.

Alou and Frederico didn't talk for quite a few days after that. The pain was still too raw for Alou. Her young charge kept up his chores, staying painfully quiet and usually a distance away from his mean brothers.

There was plenty of work to do on the rancho. With the killing season in full swing every able-bodied man was being used to round up cattle and prepare the hides for drying.

$$\approx 5 \approx$$

Several weeks later, after the slaughter had ended, Frederico resurrected his quest to learn Alou's native ways. He hated to pry but he had to know what happened when the missionary soldiers came back. His father and brothers had given him only one side of the story. From what he had seen and heard there was much more to know.

"Alou, you once mentioned that your whole village had been taken to work on the mission. How did they get away with that? Didn't your chief have a plan to save his village?" Frederico asked, bothered by the native's docile surrender.

"No, Frederico, we were talked into going by our chief. If only we had listened to my father. He tried desperately to convince our chief to prepare for an attack. Our chief disregarded the warning signs. He wanted to cooperate peacefully with the newcomers. My father once told me the frustrating story of how it came to be. This is what he said to me.

One day the chief stood near the village storehouse.

It was filled with acorns. His two wives stood beside him waiting for his instructions. The chief was preparing to determine how much food was left in this storehouse. They needed enough for all the villagers, visitors, and needy people.

"Let's see what we have left," the chief told his young wives. He peered in and saw the room was nearly filled with brown acorns. To get a better idea of how many remained he flattened the top with his arm.

"There is enough," the chief determined. Of course they couldn't live on acorns alone. They also needed fresh meat. He never worried about this because of the abundance of game in the area. Herds of deer grazed in small groups and scores of rabbits nibbled timidly on the edge of the brush. Along the wide sandy beaches clams by the thousands lay exposed by the relentless wave action. Fish teamed in the cold blue sea. Their village had always been blessed with an abundance of food.

Dust rose from the earth where two children wrestled. In the distance a solitary man approached. It was Paha, my father. He drew close to the chief, waiting patiently for him to finish instructing his wives. The look on Paha's face troubled the chief.

"May I have a word with you?" Paha asked. A lifelong friend, the chief smiled broadly and responded,

"Paha, why the long face? What's the matter? Please tell me what's troubling you."

The perplexed look on Paha's face sounded an alarm deep within the chief's heart. Paha, normally a jovial fellow full of life and happiness, never seemed so antagonized.

"My friend and leader, I have some very disturbing news for you. The newcomers from the south have begun rounding up villagers for work details," Paha said, adding,

"They were not given a choice. Fighting broke out and some of our neighbors died. Worse yet, the word is they will be coming to our village next. What do you want to do?"

The chief's face grew long. His deeply furrowed brow pulled tight. For years the padres and their soldiers occupied a small portion of the village land. Several times in the past they had visited his village and spoke to them about their god. They persuaded some of the more impressionable villagers to leave with them. Up to this point they had always asked voluntarily for new converts. If this message was true, they had stopped asking and now were forcing natives to toil like slaves.

The chief searched his mind for an answer. Maybe if they shared their food the soldiers would leave them alone. Perhaps they would realize the advantages of having us as good neighbors. We could all work together for the common good. The chief kept trying to work out a mutual working relationship in his mind. It wasn't easy. The newcomer's ways were so different from theirs. When they spoke of their god they tended to disregard the native gods, angering the good spirits who looked over his village. He was concerned the mission padres would turn his people away from all they've known. With hope fading his only chance remained with making the newcomers their friends and allies.

"Have you any other news that might make sense of this?" The chief asked.

Paha could only shake his head forlornly.

"There is nothing more," Paha told him, adding,

"What are we going to do?" as his voice faded to a whisper.

The chief thought silently for a few seconds then told

Paha,

"Pass the word. We must accept the newcomers as friends. We must strive to win them over. This way we can all live our chosen ways without fear of the others."

Paha was not convinced the peaceful solution would work.

"Listen to me, the soldiers are not our friends. They are under orders from the padres to round up the native people for mission work. They will not give us a choice. Already men have died trying to protect their loved ones. I say we prepare for war. If they come and try to forcibly take us we'll be ready. If they do come in peace we can accept them into our hearts and live as friends. But that is a long shot," Paha argued.

The chief was not listening. His decision was final. He would work out a compromise with the newcomers to insure the continuation of his tribe. The great spirits would protect them he reasoned.

Paha stormed away, grief stricken with the chief's final word, an image of doom etched into his mind.

"This is the story of how my people ceased to exist as guardians of the land. Frederico, there was nothing we could do. Now, after many decades as slaves, our people have lost sight of what is rightfully theirs," Alou cried softly.

"Alou, tell me the rest of the story. I have to know what happened to your father Paha and the rest of your family," Frederico begged.

"Forty years ago my father Paha went to his tule hut and prepared for war while the rest of the village milled about waiting for the soldiers to come. He had a surprise for them if they stepped too close. Hidden in Paha's mass of shoulder length black hair was a flint knife. It had a razor-honed edge, sharpened by precision flaking. Like most of the remaining men of the village Paha always kept his dagger in place. In all likelihood the soldiers would not be coming peacefully and he wanted to be ready to defend himself and his family. My father had heard that the day before a fight had broken out in a neighboring village between the mission soldiers and the tribal elders. Three members of that tribe were slain by the angry soldiers. Many more would have been murdered had not all the men in the village jumped into the fray. Their sinew backed bows and arrows took the soldiers by surprise, resulting in their retreat. Bloodied but intact the soldiers vowed to return.

Paha called our family together to explain the dangerous situation. Nervously, we gathered in the small clearing by our hut. Paha looked up from deep despair and saw the faces of his past and future. He had survived many brushes with death during his lifetime and was not afraid to face it again.

"Listen to me!" Paha demanded angrily.

"We will ask the spirits of our ancestors to rise up and strike down these soldiers. They will give us the power to drive the invaders from our sacred land. We need to prepare for war. We need to be ready!" Paha told our extended family, friends, and the tribal chief.

The chief looked at his friend with great pride. No fear resided in this native man and his brave spirit was unwilling to lie down and give up. Paha tugged on some of the long strands of hair that cascaded over his ears. His hair framed clear black eyes and a mischievous soul. Slowly he started to speak again but was interrupted by the chief who was worried about his alarming remarks.

"Paha, you're dealing with the lives of our village. What you're asking us to do will surely result in our annihilation.

We don't stand a chance. If the soldiers want us we must go with them and be allowed to save our lives. We must survive as a people at all costs!" The chief demanded.

The chief's statement left Paha speechless. For many years Paha had been a trusted advisor but on this matter they could not find common ground.

"Paha, your heart is full of courage. There is no question about that. But my allegiance rests with saving the lives of our people. I can't allow us to perish and be forgotten."

The chief spoke from his heart. He had always been a wonderful friend to my father. His call for a peaceful solution showed where his logic rested but Paha knew deep in his heart that the chief was making a mistake.

Nearby, several children laughed and played with a stinkbug crawling in the dirt. Paha wondered what would happen to these rosy-cheeked kids. The children might be able to adapt under mission rule but he knew his tribal brothers could not.

Filled with courage my father asked the chief for his support.

"Please, I ask that you follow my lead in the days ahead. Don't let the fear of death control your destiny. Let's proudly carry ourselves into the future," Paha pleaded.

"Paha, we choose to live. Please come with us if the soldiers come. We need you. Your family needs you. I need you," the chief begged with considerable emotion.

"No!" Paha declared resolutely.

"I will never give up my ways. I'd rather be dead among the spirits then to live life in restraint at the mission," he concluded, too emotionally upset to consider the consequences.

Paha defiantly left the group and walked away in

disgust.

"You'll die Paha!" The chief cried.

"Don't go. Stay with us!" He added as the tears began to flow from the chief's eyes.

Paha turned and said,

"So be it. At least I'll die a man of my words."

Paha wondered how many more days they would have together. As fate would have it, today would be their last. Paha desperately wanted to assure his family everything would be all right. He knew this could never be and feared the screams of the captured would haunt him for decades.

Thousands of years had passed since the natives established their permanent home in the area. In a matter of days their entire village was under siege. Paha wondered why his village had been singled out. Why hadn't the chief listened to his warnings? Could his tribe have offended the spirits? All kinds of crazy scenarios played out in his mind. It was as though his world was collapsing around him.

The loud crying of a hungry baby caught Paha's attention. How many more would follow suit in the days ahead.

The next day the missionary soldiers came. Surprising them at daybreak they overran the limited resistance within minutes. Paha fought fiercely against the intruders. His wife joined in the skirmish, putting up the fight of her life. Sadly, she suffered a compound fracture of her leg and died an agonizing death two weeks later from gangrene. After the valiant native resistance broke down, I was taken away.

Detained briefly, Paha vowed never to surrender. In a moment of confusion Paha escaped by pulling his flint dagger from his hair and slashing his way to safety. Now alone in the wild land of his youth Paha continued to sustain himself the old native way. The last one from his village to do so."

Alou had one more thing to say but decided to wait.

"Frederico, that is all I can say today. The pain and sorrow in my heart hurts too much to continue."

"Please Alou, don't be afraid to tell me the truth. I have to know," Frederico pleaded.

"I was taken by force to La Purisima mission. The rest of our village plodded along with me, too intimidated to mount much of a protest. The next year, 1801, disease was so rampant at the mission that nearly the entire native population died.

"Frederico, after they took us to the mission I saw firsthand the horrible diseases that these newcomers had brought. They were devastating. The death rate among the children was the highest. In the crowded conditions it was very easy to catch new diseases. Most of our people had never developed a resistance to these. Names like measles, tuberculosis, syphilis, and the dreaded poxes. Not many of the natives lived more then seven or eight years. I was among the fortunate. Most of the women died from savage abuse at the hands of the soldiers. The indescribable humiliation these women and girls were forced to endure sickens me even now. Syphilis spread between the soldiers and the victims. More then half our village died directly from the particularly cruel act of rape. The men died too, in defense of the women, or from the spreading tentacles of that demon syphilis. Only my age, ten, spared me from the depraved acts of the soldiers.

Those of us who were not killed by disease endured profound changes in our lifestyle, diet and beliefs. We died collectively as a tribe that year. Only a few are left today.

For this reason I believe life has a purpose for me. There is a greater glory in store for me. Part of that involves you Frederico. My heart sinks every time I see you endure the tedious harassment from your brothers. But you alone must find something in yourself before you can deal with it. I will be there for you when that happens, I promise," Alou sincerely revealed.

Frederico was stunned by her remarks. Alou's wisdom was right. Someday he'd have to gather the courage to change the situations with his brothers. He just didn't feel like he had the fortitude yet.

Frederico squirmed in his spot.

"Alou, why didn't enough brave souls stand up to fight the abuses," the outraged boy blurted.

"Why didn't the padres stop the soldiers," he gasped, profoundly effected by the tales of pain.

Alou hesitated momentarily before telling of the revolt led by her father.

"There was one man, Frederico, who dared to challenge the mission authority. That man was Paha, my father. He was fifty years old by then and living in the old village, biding his time for the right opportunity to strike," Alou whispered, more out of respect then anything else.

"Your father must have been quite some man," Frederico replied, adding,

"It's too bad he was never given the chance to lead your people through the crisis."

"Oh, but he did try to save us. Once he led a revolt against the padres and their soldiers," Alou related.

Pretty soon the whole story of the revolt spilled from Alou's lips.

"Paha's rebellion constituted the last attempt by our

people to shed the shackles of mission servitude. It worked for a while but not long enough."

"Tell me what happened," Frederico inquired, in awe of the tales of bravery.

"Weeks before my father's revolt Paha secretly contacted the leaders of the native group at the mission. My father provided the weapons they needed to overwhelm the small contingent of soldiers.

On that fateful day, Feb. 21, 1824, some of our native men surprised the six soldiers who were assigned to La Purisima mission. The battle was short lived. The mission soldiers were overrun after killing one of our men. In the heat of the battle four travelers were also killed. Natives from the Santa Barbara mission had staged a similar attack at their mission that day and were fleeing a great force of soldiers. They stopped and helped us.

During the battle they barricaded themselves inside the mission buildings, fortifying themselves with two swivel guns. They cut slits to shoot their weapons but these tactics didn't work for long. Unfortunately, my father's rebellion didn't last.

Almost a full month later a force of one hundred soldiers came and demanded our surrender. We wouldn't give up so they attacked us. It was a bloodbath. Sixteen of our men were killed, scores wounded. Later, seven of our native men were executed and the rest, around twelve, were sent to prisons for long terms. My father would have been the eighth man executed had I not cut his bindings. He remained the only man from our village to escape and make it to freedom. Dejected and beaten my father walked back to the village and tried to live out the remaining years of his life in peace," Alou revealed. She was still hurting from the memory but realized Frederico needed to know her story.

"After the revolt the remaining natives continued the ways of the mission. All those years in servitude had wiped out most of their past native memories.

As one of the only survivors from the diseases the soldiers passed to our people, I was thought to be very powerful and thus I was watched very closely. They were worried I would attempt to organize another revolt to drive out the missionaries. They kept us uninformed and stupid, refusing to teach us even the simplest of things."

Frederico was full of questions. They spewed out of his mouth like a fountain. Alou was more then obliged to answer them. By telling her story she was healing wounds deep in her soul.

"After we were indoctrinated by the padres they put us to work around the missions. We were called neophytes. Our naked skin made them uncomfortable so they issued us coarse shirts to wear. Our sleeping habits were no longer acceptable so the padres exercised control over all our daily life. Worst of all were the clothes. They itched very badly.

I was put in a nunnery right away. The padres locked all the single women ages eleven and up every night. When the sun came up we were awakened and taken to mass. Language instruction and breakfast followed. They would work us very hard after breakfast. We were expected to do the labor without complaint and always follow the rules exactly.

Sundays were a day of rest and every once in a great while they would allow us to venture into the hills, even to our old villages if close by. My village was gone by then, burned to the ground by rogue soldiers. The old villagers were killed off by disease or maltreatment. I was the lone survivor with the exception of my father Paha. He was a free eagle spirit that could never be tamed.

I started in the weaving shop where I helped spin the wool. All the clothes of the mission were made there. Blankets, shirts, pants, we did it all. The shop next door made leather jackets and moccasins. Eventually, I learned how to make those too. When the padres saw how easily I took to the Spanish language they made me an interpreter. Later, my fondness for kids drew me to the nursery. Ever since then, I've worked with children, raising them with the hope they would be able to stand on their own two feet. Frederico, of all the kids I have cared for you are my favorite.

When the harvest began all of us worked together to bring in the crops. Men and women worked together. The mission way of life became the only way we knew. The old ways were quickly forgotten or prohibited by the padres," Alou sighed. She needed to take a breather. All this talk about her life was wearing her out.

"Alou, that's enough to think about for now. Tell me one last thing. Why did the missions break up? They seemed to be so powerful. How did they lose that so fast?" Frederico questioned, unable to shut up.

"We were declared free in 1827 but that was a charade. Six years later, in 1833, the process really began. The missions were broken up and control shifted to the great ranchos. We went from one master to another. In the last seven years our numbers have fallen to almost nothing. I'm sure your generation will be the last to witness our great native ways," Alou recited wearily. She continued with one last observation of her painful life.

"Rancho life has been just as hard. We changed our ways and adapted to the ranchos but the death of our culture was the price we paid. It was either adapt or die so we chose to survive."

Alou had said enough. She stopped talking and left Frederico deep in thought. Completely involved in the tragic saga that had destroyed a culture eons old.

꙳ ◊ ꙳

Days passed as Frederico endured daily drudgery and humiliation. Even his sleeping area had been compromised. Miguel and Carlos had overflowed into his living area leaving him limited space to rest. Set deep in the corner, Frederico's darkened cubby provided only enough legroom to lay bent like a pretzel. Boxing him in, the terrible twins laid claim to his former area. In his new spot Frederico could stand but only because he was barely four feet tall. A small bookcase took up a little space against the cool, plastered adobe wall. The boy had managed to fill the dusty shelves with old musty smelling books from his father's library. Among them were examples of romance, history, and adventure novels. All these books opened doors in his mind. Offering an escape from the common drudgery that is life. Stolen minutes alone with only his imagination as a companion. Frederico relished the chance to rise above his misery and place himself in a tranquil environment.

Long, with a low ceiling, and musty from mildew, the

rancho boys occupied the entire half-story above the main kitchen. Yummy smells of baking bread drifted up into the room making their quarters quite homey.

Frederico adjusted his pants with a hitch and a jerk, and plodded down the stairs to breakfast. His oldest brother Juan was already sitting at the table.

"Hey sleepy head, have something to drink," Juan coaxed, smiling gently. He handed a cup of cool water to Frederico and patted him on the back.

"Your brothers left early this morning. Father had something for them to do over at the blacksmith shop. I think they're putting things in their rightful places. What do you say we make the rounds together? We don't get a chance to talk very often. You seem kind of down and I was wondering if you wanted to tell me about it?" Juan suggested tenderly.

Frederico wiggled his nose like he did when he was happy and responded,

"Juan, I'd love to talk to you. For a big brother you're pretty nice. I just wish Carlos and Miguel would follow your example."

Juan, twenty years old, was well liked by everyone. Being the oldest boy he was showered with gifts and affection. Heir and future leader of the rancho, Juan certainly acted the part. He was serious in nature, not one to waste time bullying others.

Frederico was very fond of Juan. He looked up to him and proudly bragged about him. A natural born leader Juan led most of the rancho cattle operations. His father knew he had a worthy successor in his son Juan and took the young man on most business trips. No time was leftover for the other sons. The youngest, Frederico, was lucky to spend five minutes with his dad a week. The rest of the time the Captain would sidestep Frederico's questions, ignoring him.

"Okay, I'll meet you outside by the barn in five minutes. We need to check the status of things. You can take notes for me," Juan suggested.

Whistling a snappy tune Juan slipped out the front door and walked confidently over to the barn. He nodded good morning to everyone along the way. The natives, treated with kindness and good grace by Juan, responded favorably to his good nature.

Frederico wanted to let Alou know where he was going so he ran through the house looking for her.

"Alou, Alou," he called, poking his head into the big room where all the different grains were stored. Not there. Down the hall and around the corner he looked in the milk room where a native girl churned butter.

"Please," Frederico tried to motion.

"Alou? Alou? Where is she?" He said, holding his hand out and lifting his shoulders up to express his question.

"Oh," the young native woman said and pointed her calloused finger in the direction of the kitchen.

"Alou, Alou!" The butter churner said, trying to direct him. Frederico was a favorite of most of the native servants. Her friend Alou had told her of his curiosity about native ways. The small boy finally deciphered what the butter churner was saying.

Frederico responded,

"Thank you," and skipped to the kitchen.

"Alou, are you here?" He called.

"Frederico, are you looking for me?" Alou inquired, busy gathering food for a meal, as she stepped into sight.

"Yes, I'm going to help Juan with his chores today. He's my buddy," Frederico chortled.

"Very good, my young man. Did you tell your father?" Alou wondered.

"No, he's with the twins. They're sorting things in the blacksmith shop. He won't care. He never cares what I do," Frederico sniffed.

"Okay, I'll see you later. We can talk," Alou said as she carried a large tray of food into the dining room. The rancho house had extra large rooms to accommodate the growing rancho family and multitude of servants. The front wing had one and a half stories. Upstairs there was one large room. Juan, the twins Miguel and Carlos, and Frederico all had their sleeping quarters up there. A narrow set of wooden steps descended into the front entry.

One side wing contained the living areas and dining room. The other side wing housed the master bedroom and the girl's bedroom. One more side room doubled as a storage area and guest room.

All the rooms opened up into a grand courtyard with fountains, garden terraces and arched sitting areas. Partially tiled for dancing, many parties had been hosted there by Frederico's family.

Frederico ran out the back door and around the west wing. Ahead he saw Juan talking to several mounted vaqueros by the barn.

"Juan, here I am, let me help," the young boy eagerly offered.

"Okay little guy. These men are giving me their orders for supplies. Help me write them down," Juan mentioned. Frederico whipped out a piece of paper and a pencil and wrote everything down.

The rest of the morning, Frederico followed Juan around, taking down orders, tallying supplies, checking the progress in the shop. They went down the row of shops and outbuildings situated across the old King's road. Starting at the barn, moving to the candle and soap room, the furniture warehouse, lumber storeroom, and then to the saddle shop. Frederico loved this room. The smell of worked leather always tickled his senses.

From there the brothers moved to the big room with the loom. The looms were operated by a very busy group of native girls. Yarn flew through the loops. Serapes were being made today and they were so finely woven they could hold water. A lesser grade of cloth, yerga, was being prepared for the natives. Another room held the spinning wheels and the carpenter's room adjoined that one.

They approached the blacksmith shop but turned away when Juan noticed Frederico's anxious look. Inside, Miguel and Carlos did work that brought beads of sweat to their pudgy brows. Their unhappy scowls were not a good sign. Surely this would lead to another humiliating round of teasing for Frederico.

Juan knew the cutting effect it had on his sensitive brother Frederico. There was no need to put him through that today. As long as he had the time he would spare his youngest brother this fate.

The last places they needed to check were the shoe shop on the edge of the mesa and the small room with the brandy still.

They sauntered over to the cluster of rooms near the creek bottom. Everything checked out at the shoe shop so they went to the still. They passed the arroyo where the vegetable garden was laid out. Beyond that the still hid behind the windmill water well.

A few feet from the entrance Juan stopped suddenly and

held his fingers to his lips. Clearly audible inside were the sounds of someone laughing. Long, cackling expressions of glee. Juan tiptoed over, looked through a crack in a sidewall and saw one of his vaqueros chugging newly distilled brandy.

"Hey Humberto! Get out of there. Look at yourself you slobbering drunk. You ought to be ashamed of yourself. Go over by the big sycamore and sleep it off. Here, let me help you. Frederico, give us a hand here."

The two of them helped Humberto to his feet, deftly supporting his staggering body. Down by the creek dead leaves had built up, mercifully forming soft spots for the intoxicated man to sleep on.

Juan had a huge dose of compassion for all his men. Some of them had problems but Juan made it a policy to never beat a man down because of it. This tolerant attitude went a long ways towards building respect within his crew of vaqueros and was one of Juan's finest traits. Frederico tried to mimic his brother in this way. It made a difference from what Frederico could see.

They finished the walk through and went back to the house where they ate some carne seca and parted ways. Juan needed to work out on the range tending to some cattle and Frederico wanted to sustain his happy mood after his time with Juan.

Left alone at the house Frederico soon became the target of the twin's sweaty wrath. Their father had left Carlos and Miguel shortly after Juan had rode out to the range. Before he left he gave the twins strict orders to fix a cartwheel before he got back. Supposedly, he had also told them to enlist Frederico's help in the effort.

"You creep, where did you go today with Juan? Didn't

you see we needed help in the blacksmith shop! If father hadn't been there you would have been mincemeat," Miguel snapped, still aching from his earlier chores.

Frederico froze at the sound of his tormented voice.

"Uh, ooooh," Frederico gasped under his breath. Miguel walked over and stood in front of Frederico, who trembled visibly in his presence. Without warning he pushed Frederico over the hunched body of Carlos who had snuck up behind the boy and crouched behind him.

Frederico went flying head over heels, landing solidly on his shoulders and jamming his thin neck in the process.

"Uggg!" Frederico groaned, too petrified to cry for fear of further punishment.

The twins rolled on the ground hysterically, somehow finding their brother's pain extremely funny. They stopped their cackling long enough to order Frederico to stand up and apologize to them for making them laugh so hard that they nearly wet their pants.

"Sorry," Frederico muttered.

"What, I can't hear you!" They both screamed in his face.

"I'm sorry, I'm sorry, please leave me alone. Just leave me alone," Frederico begged, in tears.

"Hey crybaby, you gonna cry again, come on, cry for us you dirty weasel. Crybaby, crybaby!" Miguel spewed in his face, as his spittle flew straight into Frederico's eye.

Frederico sucked up whatever dignity he had left in his scrawny body and held back his tears. It took all his concentration to pull it off.

A passing vaquero startled the twins, temporarily halting their abuse. When the man passed they continued their tirade against Frederico.

"We'll let you go for now you big whiner. Besides, we have a job for you. Father told us he wants you to repair this cartwheel by the time he gets back. You better put a pep in your step if you want to finish on time," Miguel hyped.

The cartwheel in question had broken off near the hub.

"Father wants you to chisel out the hub and prep it for another beam," Miguel ordered.

Frederico plodded, head down, to the blacksmith shop, stopping inside for a second to retrieve a chisel and hammer. This was going to be a big job. The axle hole had a six-inch diameter piece of broken wood wedged tightly inside and the only way to clear it out was to chisel it clean.

Frederico sat sadly next to the cartwheel and began the long tedious process. A few feet away his brothers stood on a stump and started tossing pebbles at him, keeping score according to where they hit him.

Frederico ignored them while he examined the three-foot wide sycamore wheel. Rough hewn from a suitably sized tree trunk and cut into slabs the wheel had been whittled down to four inches thick. It was huge and incredibly heavy. Far too heavy to handle alone. He needed help from the twins but knew there was no chance of that happening.

Off to the side of the blacksmith shop the broken cart sat cockeyed. Built very wide and close to the ground it took a major bungle to overturn. Used mainly to carry goods, and rarely, passengers, the cart was hitched by yoke to oxen with rawhide thongs.

"Ouch!" Frederico remarked loudly as a pebble hit Frederico right behind his left ear.

The twins waited for a smart remark but Frederico kept quiet, not wanting to muddy the waters.

"Watch this," Miguel said as he elbowed Carlos. He

picked up a whole handful of gravel sized pebbles and threw them high in the air over Frederico. The shower of rocks hit the boy in the back and shoulders and sent Frederico over the edge. All his pain and frustration came shrieking out of his soul.

"Stop it you bully! You mean evil boy! Stop it!" Frederico screamed at the top of his lungs.

The twins were startled by the high pitched scream. They rocked back on their heels dumbfounded.

"You bastard! I hate you! I hate you! You're making my life so hard! Why don't you just leave me alone?" Frederico wailed, crying extremely loud.

His screaming brought several servants running to his side, certain he had been seriously injured. The twins were shocked and embarrassed by the scene. Scrambling to their feet, they high tailed it back to the blacksmith shop, hustling to catch up with their chores before their dad got back.

Frederico sat on the wheel sobbing uncontrollably, his shoulders heaving and shuddering with each protracted sob. Pretty soon Alou came and wrapped her loving arms around the boy. She kept squeezing until the tears stopped then helped the boy to his feet and back to the house. Alou took him upstairs and tucked him into his bed. Her heart was in despair, aching for his crushed soul. She knew she could not control the twins and cared not to tread in those troubled waters. Alou sat by Frederico and stroked his sweaty head while trying to calm him down. She waited by his bed in case Miguel came back. Later, she would wake him for the rest of the chores. For now, though, he needed rest to revitalize his defenses.

$$\approx 7 \approx$$

Later, Alou came back and woke Frederico up. It wasn't quite 2:00 in the afternoon and Frederico needed to get busy with the rest of his chores. His daily list included feeding the chickens, keeping all the animals locked up, and helping in the various spinning and weaving rooms. Heavy work was imposed on the natives, but Frederico was expected to assist wherever he could.

"Wake up Frederico," Alou said gingerly.

"It's time to get up," she repeated.

"Your chores need to be done before the sun goes down."

"Ok Alou, I'm awake. I haven't forgotten. Thanks for letting me sleep. I'm feeling better now," replied the beaten rancho boy.

Frederico went outside and performed his duties without problems. He said nothing to the busy workers around him. Still in a deeply depressed mood he walked around like a zombie drifting through the motions.

He finished his chores and shuffled back to the house. Alou waited for him by the courtyard. He trod right past her, too exhausted to talk.

Alou followed Frederico, keeping a short distance behind him, mindful of his need for personal space. When they reached Frederico's room he went in and sat on his bedding. Alou came over and sat next to him.

"I don't want to talk about it," the boy moaned, adding,

"It's just not worth it!"

Alou said nothing, content to sit and listen. She let him stew for a while. Before long Frederico spoke out, changing the subject, desperate to block the pain from his mind.

"Alou, tell me what you like to do. You know, in your spare time. Sometimes I see you and the other native ladies playing some kind of game."

Alou hesitated, then said,

"I like to gamble. We play games with native dice. Do you want to learn how?"

"What do you gamble?" Frederico asked, knowing that gambling usually involved betting money.

"We use strings of shell money as currency. I used to have piles of strings but the gambling spirits have not been favorable to me lately. I made them by taking olivella shells and breaking off pieces roughly of similar size. Using a chert drill we made holes in the center and strung a string through the middle. Then we would roll them on sandstone rocks until all of them were rounded to a uniform size.

Our native unit of currency was a string of shell beads wrapped once around the hand. This was the standard value of measurement in our territory. Besides gambling we used the shell bead money for trading and offerings to the spirits.

Most of the trade we engaged in involved some transfers of shell beads. They were valuable," Alou explained, adding,

"Here, let me get some strings to show you."

She fished around in her pockets before pulling out two long strings of shell money. The rounded shells were smaller then Frederico expected.

"These are the only strands I have left so please be careful with them," Alou stated proudly.

Frederico took the strings of shell bead money in his hands and slowly ran the strands through his fingers. The consistent size and shape remained remarkably even. He looked at them for a second then handed them back to his native nanny.

"Thanks for showing me," he told her.

Alou rarely had time to discuss her own personal pleasures. Thrilled, she stuffed the strings in a small bag and tied the fiber strings closed.

She was excited, almost edgy. All this talk of shell bead money stoked her gambling bug. From another pocket she pulled out dice and began to explain her favorite game. She said,

"Lets play, come on, I'll show you how."

Alou practiced rolling the dice and tried to get the boy interested. Frederico seemed slightly blasé about the whole matter. Perhaps if she played a while he would show some interest.

Alou's native dice were hollowed out walnut shells filled with asphaltum for weight. Halved, the dark walnut shells were decorated with shell beads. One side was flat and the other side was rounded.

Alou shook the dice in her hands, calling out the combo she wanted,

"Come on, here we go again, give me the numbers," Alou yakked as she tossed the modified nutshells across a winnowing tray.

"Yea!" She called out, excited by the outcome of the roll.

"Again!" She called out as she tossed the dice onto the flat, coiled tray.

Forgotten for the moment was Frederico. He watched her get excited about the brief demonstration but couldn't get into the flow. The interest wasn't there. The poor boy's spirit couldn't respond to her uplifting efforts. He watched her politely for a few minutes then closed his eyes and replayed all the terrible things his brothers had done to him recently. They were his flesh and blood. Didn't they love him? The question burned in his brain, frying a spot that was already sore.

Alou saw Frederico with his teary eyes closed. Unfortunately, her gambling game had not diverted attention away from his mountain of problems.

"Would you like to give it a try?" Alou asked gently.

Alou didn't wait for his answer. She dropped the dice back into her pocket, slid the winnowing tray under a tule mat and started to talk again. Her concentrated attention seemed to have a healing effect on Frederico. The tears stopped and he straightened up slightly.

Alou knew the boy needed some loving attention. Something his father or mother, God help heal her tortured mind, never gave. With his mother gone Frederico needed extra reassurance that everything was going to be all right. The father did what he could, at least initially, but quickly became obsessed with the rancho business. Poor Frederico, had it not been for Alou's constant nurturing, might have wasted away all together.

Frederico's mother's unexpected malaise threw the whole family into disarray. The timing of her sudden illness, two weeks after the move from Santa Barbara, could not have been worse. Still ill, the sanitarium refused to release her. That had been almost two years ago. She probably wouldn't be back anytime soon. Alou felt sorry for the boy. Childless, she had taken in Frederico and treated him as if he were her own.

Something needed to be done to boost his spirits. Perhaps a fun game played outdoors in the bright sunshine with the other kids. Alou thought about all the fun games she used to play before the soldiers came. One stood out among all the others.

"Shinny!" Alou said out loud.

A few hours later Alou rounded up all the kids on the rancho and instructed them on the rules of the game. Frederico brightened up considerably when she suggested he play the game with the others. Alou quickly selected two teams of kids. Both teams surrounded a circle scratched in the middle of the field.

Somewhere in the circle of sand, buried inches below the surface, was the puck. Made from a ball shaped piece of wood the puck was the central piece of the game. Each team of four players carried a stick three to four feet long, curved slightly at the bottom. The curved part of the stick was used to bat the puck towards the opposite ends of the field where goal lines were marked about ten feet wide. The object of the game was to strike the ball continuously until you moved it across the opposing goal line.

Alou stood nearby going over last second instructions with one of the kids.

"Is everybody ready?" She called out in Spanish to the rancho kids. They all shook their heads yes.

"Okay, go! Find the puck!" She yelled, in her high squeaky voice. On cue everybody started digging through the sandy circle searching for the puck. One of the twins, Miguel, knocked the puck to the surface with a quick sweeping motion, and the game was on.

Delighted squeals of joy filled the air. Sticks were flying with reckless abandon. One of the kids whacked it really hard, nearly the full length of the makeshift field. In the mad dash for the puck, Frederico sprinted to the front of the pack. He freed himself from the rest of the kids and was racing to attain the hitting position. The twins caught up to Frederico and purposely thrust their sticks at his legs. They missed the first few times, then Miguel succeeded in catching him between the legs just as he was winding up to shoot the winning goal.

Frederico tripped and fell face first into the dirt. The impact knocked the air out of him and he lay there stunned, unable to catch his breath.

The rest of the kids continued after the puck. Miguel reached it first and instead of hitting it towards the opposite end, scooped it up with his hands and dashed off the playing field. Carlos joined him and laughed at the rest of the kids who stood there on the field, perturbed at the twins.

"Hey, where are you going?" One of the other kids asked.

"Give us the puck," they requested loudly, somewhat irritated that the game would end so abruptly.

"No way, catch us if you can, but I wouldn't try it. The first one who does is going to get a stick to the teeth," warned Miguel menacingly.

The other kids knew his reputation as a bully and realized the folly of trying to get the puck back. They grumbled for a few seconds then threw their sticks to the ground and trudged home with their high spirits deflated by the idiotic twins.

Frederico lay writhing on the ground, struggling to sustain a regular breathing rhythm. Alou stayed on the sidelines exhorting the boy,

"Get up, get up!" Her mood was angry. The twins had promised they would be nice to Frederico. She never should have believed them. Miguel was evil and disturbed and Carlos did everything Miguel told him to do, no matter how mean. She could never trust them again.

Frederico picked himself up and walked gingerly down to the creek bottom. He sat on a rock next to the flowing stream and stared at the trickling waters. That last trip to the ground had effectively knocked the wind and spirit out of Frederico at the same time.

"Frederico! Frederico!" Alou cried

She went to him but stopped short of where he sat. She could tell Frederico was too distraught to cry and too frustrated to talk, even with her.

Alou felt absolutely terrible. What she had conceived as a way to cheer the boy up had deteriorated into something far worse. In a very real way, she felt responsible for the situation. Worst of all, she had exhausted all of her own ideas in the quest to make Frederico happy and loved.

Alou decided at that moment to take drastic measures. Only one person she knew could possibly have the wisdom to assist Frederico in his search for true happiness. Paha, her wise native father.

≈ 8 ≈

Alou never revealed her father's existence for almost forty years. His life in the dunes was kept a secret. She saw him only three or four times a year, at best, and was committed to ensuring his dream of living out the remainder of his life in true native fashion. But lately, she had noticed her father was out of sync, profoundly occupied with his own place.

Paha openly agonized over who would carry on the native ways. The missionaries had ripped that knowledge from the converts, and as far as he knew, no other natives still inhabited the numerous villages along the coast. It had been over a decade since he had seen another native person in the wild. Wisdom needed to be passed on, including the knowledge of the spirits and their native ways. This information was too valuable and important to be lost to the ages. Paha asked the spirits to send someone with an insatiable thirst for knowledge, someone who could understand the significance.

Alou also felt the same way. The accumulated knowledge of her people must survive. After Frederico's mother left the rancho Alou chose the boy as a noble recipient of her native knowledge. Frederico's natural curiosity and emphatic nature made him the only candidate suitable for this great responsibility.

Alou hoped Paha would see those attributes and take the boy under his wing while helping him in the transitions of life.

When the others gathered in the house Alou slipped into the woods on a borrowed horse and rode straight for Paha's secret location. There wasn't a minute to lose. Alou found Paha lying down in the hut Frederico had broken into previously.

"Are you sick Father?" Alou asked concerned about his idle pose.

"No, my dear, only sad and concerned. Who will care when I'm gone?" He asked out of the blue.

"Why, I'll be here," Alou tenderly reminded him.

"I'll care, I promise you. Don't worry Paha."

"No, Alou. I mean who will care about our culture and our long and fantastic history once I'm gone. Much of what remains rests only in my head. Who will take this gift from me and carry it forward?"

"I know someone Father, a special young boy who is worthy of this gift and so much more. I think you know whom I'm talking about. His name is Frederico and he's been chosen by my spirit to receive my gifts. He possesses the right mind to absorb your knowledge and cherish it and make it a vital part of his inner soul."

Paha knew of the boy. Alou had talked frequently about him the last two years. He was the same boy who had stumbled into his life with the discovery of the hut. The same boy who had taken his feather blankets then returned them and even helped fix his damaged hut.

On that fateful day, even from a distance, Paha saw something special in the boy. An aura usually reserved for great leaders and intellectuals. Perhaps Frederico was the special spirit he sought. All signs pointed positively towards the boy and Paha knew he could help him. Confidence and bold courage could be gained, fortifying him for the future. Skills the boy would need to survive in bad times.

"Alou, for forty years, I've lived out here by myself. During this time the spirits have been good to me by always providing a bountiful supply of food and water. The only thing I've missed has been the company of others. I would love to have someone to talk to and teach our ways. If your good heart feels this way about him I will open myself up and teach him. I can make him understand the importance of standing on his own two feet. My teachings will give him the courage to right what is wrong in his life. Bring him to me Alou. Let's see what the spirits have in store for him," Paha calmly directed.

Alou wanted to shout for joy when she heard Paha's decision. Hope grew in her heart for Frederico's successful transition. Alou left Paha in the old village, confident the vast knowledge of her father would lead the boy from his despair.

Frederico was still lying down when Alou came home. She went straight upstairs and roused him from his slumber.

"Frederico, I have something important to tell you. You must promise to never reveal this secret to anyone else. It is very important that you understand this. Frederico, clear your sleepy head and listen to me. It's critical that you keep this to yourself. You must not tell another living soul," she said very seriously.

Frederico sat up and wiped the dried tears from his eyes. What is it he wondered? What kind of secret does she have?

"Alou, you intrigue me with the urgency of your tone. What are you talking about? Please tell me. You have my sincere word that I will never tell a soul," Frederico declared. The boy knew this would be easy since no one cared about what he had to say anyway.

Alou looked deep into the boy's eyes and knew she could trust him completely.

"Frederico, I have a secret you should know. Remember when I spoke of Paha, my wonderful father, the native man who stubbornly resisted all change. My great father, the man I said I would gladly die for. He's living Frederico and, best yet, he has agreed to meet with you and show you the ways of our people. Frederico, remember the fire-lights you saw dancing in the dunes. That was my father calling to the spirits for guidance. You were the first newcomer in forty years to find his tule hut. The spirits must have directed you to take that shortcut through the dunes that fateful day, Now it was only a matter of time before someone finally came for my father. He had no guarantee you wouldn't tell everybody about the hut. He expected hordes of rancho men to come and take every last object of value, including his long life.

When you came back the next day with me to fix the hut and return the blankets he realized you were someone special. Frederico, he has no one left but me in this world. He yearns for the right spirit to leave his vast knowledge to. We think you could be that person. Meet with him. Feel the power of his native spirits. As our tribal shaman, my father has been entrusted with the secrets of our universe. When he dies, those secrets, our ways, will be lost forever. That is what he fears most. Help him put that fear behind him."

Frederico's ears turned so red he thought they might burst. Alou's revelation had taken him completely by surprise. Her clarity left no room for misunderstanding. The man in the dunes was real and wanted to meet him. This was too good to be true. In all his years he had never heard something so inspiring and moving. Of course he would like to meet him.

"I'm flattered he would consider me for such an important role. You know native ways interest me. Sometimes the sheer pressure of life knocks me down and the only thing that makes me want to continue is the lure of learning native knowledge. I find your ways so fascinating. The more I learn the happier I get. Please tell him yes. I would love to learn his native ways and tell him that his secrets will be safe with me, I promise," Frederico declared.

Alou glowed with pride. It was a great honor to be selected to learn the native traditions and she knew Frederico was up to it.

"We will meet with him sometime next week. He'll let me know after I tell him of your sincere acceptance," she said.

"Alou, one more thing, what did you mean when you said shaman. I've heard you say that word before. What did Paha do as shaman?" Frederico asked.

Alou was aware of the shaman's special powers but to reveal all right now would overwhelm the boy. She decided to tell him briefly about the significant position her father had occupied and the responsibilities that went with it.

"The Shaman was part of the village leadership. He teamed with the chief on all the major decisions. Man or woman could be shaman. Knowledge was the key. Through knowledge the Shaman unleashed the powers of nature. These special people interpreted the skies and the heavenly dance of the stars and they used their supernatural wisdom to influence others and help the village."

"During the winter solstice the shaman wielded the sun staff in our most important ceremony. During the festival of the sun, the shaman's great words were essential to pull the sun back for another year. You must ask my father about this. I'll interpret for you. The knowledge he needs to pass is too important to miss," Alou insisted, adding,

" You need to use every resource at your disposal to understand the native ways."

Frederico enthusiastically agreed, eager to learn from the great man and shaman who was Alou's father. With her help there was much he could gain.

"When the time is right, I'll be ready. Take me to him. I won't let either of you down," Frederico implored.

Alou left Frederico and went outside to plan the rendezvous. A lot depended on her schedule at the rancho. Using the river trail, she normally took one hour to reach the village site on horseback. Today, she would take the boy, ready or not, and she made up her mind to let nothing stand in their way.

In a hurry she gathered a few things from her living quarters and returned to find Frederico happily making his bed.

"Frederico, we need to go today. My heart tells me there is much more to this then we know. Let's go now while it's still early. I can feel the urgency in my spirit," Alou said.

"I'm ready Alou. Let's go," Frederico piped up excitedly.

They met out by the corrals. Alou didn't have a horse but she knew how to ride. Frederico was a fair rider, short of experience, but good with the horses. They slipped away along the river trail without detection.

After riding hard for an hour Frederico recognized the side trail they had forged on the way back to the village to return the blankets. The horse tracks were barely visible. They turned and rode to a nearby tree where they tied the horses and walked the rest of the way. They left no noticeable trail. Alou didn't want unintended visitors to her father's refuge. This could lead to a dangerous situation.

Nothing could have prepared Frederico for the meeting with the mystical man of legend. Alou took the boy by the hand and led him around a heavily wooded willow thicket. The dunes crept far inland here, throwing up hills of sand hundreds of feet high. Frederico didn't remember this part of the trail. The last time they had been in too much of a hurry to mark his bearings.

The tule hut appeared out of nowhere, exactly opposite from the direction they had approached from before. Alou noticed the boy's lost look and told him,

"Don't ever come in the same way twice. You might leave a trail. We don't want anyone to know my father still lives here."

Alou slowly approached the tule hut and called out her father's name,

"Paha, Paha! It's Alou and Frederico. We have come to exchange greetings of peace and harmony."

She spoke in their native dialect. The rich, powerful language impressed Frederico with its complexity.

"Paha, are you there?" She asked.

A stirring in the hut revealed an older native man of extreme power and presence. Paha stood in the doorway letting his eyes do the work.

"Father, meet Frederico. This special boy has offered to help keep our native traditions alive. Frederico, this is Paha, master of ceremonies, and great shaman. He is the last remaining member of our tribe to live the old native way," Alou proudly told him.

Frederico was speechless, not sure what to do next. He held out his hand and squeaked,

"Nice to meet you," in Spanish.

Frederico stood there with his hand out for a few seconds while Paha eyed him intently. Seeing no threat he reached out and touched the boy's fingers. The moment was priceless. They touched fingertips for about five seconds before dropping their hands and smiling broadly into each other's eyes.

Alou was pleased they had made an instantaneous spiritual connection.

Paha spoke again with Alou, inviting her and the boy to visit him tomorrow morning to see the promise of the future.

She passed the word to Frederico, who jumped nearly two feet in the air. Frederico was beaming inside. Paha must have liked him. He was glad the native man saw something in him that no one else could. These were the first positive feelings Frederico had felt in a long time. Tomorrow was only hours away. The boy wondered how he would ever sleep in anticipation of their next meeting.

$\approx 9 \approx$

The next morning Frederico and Alou left under cover of darkness. They arrived as Paha was getting up. Alou told the boy,

"Keep your questions to a minimum. Watch and see his ways first."

Paha emerged from the hut hobbling slightly. In his right hand he held an old, gnarled manzanita cane. He acknowledged them with a smile as he prepared for the day. The stout branch he leaned on had a handle on one side that was bent at an odd angle. Alou told Frederico,

"When Paha was a young man he seldom walked. He preferred to run and never considered this an inconvenience. He was known for his endurance and speed and as a result stayed in great shape. Over the years he lost this physical advantage. He suffered many injuries, the last of which left him partially crippled. Cold weather makes it worse."

Frederico motioned to Paha and gave him a friendly wave as he watched the native hobble over to the creek. The sun hadn't completely risen and there was a cold, damp chill in the air. Paha headed straight for a small pile of fine white clay piled near the edge of the water.

The old native man scooped some of the fine clay into a small bowl, mixed it with some water and began stirring it. After the coarser dirt had settled to the bottom, Paha scooped up the suspended top layer of fine clay and rubbed it vigorously into his hair. He took several more scoops of the white clay water and kept rubbing. Suds started to form and before long, his whole shaggy mane was covered in a soapy layer of fine clay. He took the remaining soapy clay and spread it evenly over his face then scrubbed with the suds. Satisfied he was clean, he dunked his head in a hollowed out part of the creek and let the water flow through his hair and around his face. He wrung his hands through his hair several times to dislodge the leftover clay, then rinsed again. Finally, he squeezed the excess water out with his hands.

Alou whispered knowingly,

"He uses the fine white clay for head lice."

Frederico took careful note of this. They watched as Paha gathered his hair in a bunch and stuck in several wood hair pens to hold it together. The pins were about eight inches long and were decorated with shell beads in an intricate mosaic.

For clothes, Paha wore a deerskin cape with a frontal bone fastener. It hung over Paha's neck and shoulders and extended down to the small of his back. Beneath this, he wore a belt of fiber netting that hung from his waist to the upper thighs. Paha wore sandals of deerskin with straps that wrapped around his feet.

Paha stood up and walked to his hut, moving better as his morning stiffness disappeared. At the base of the hut he picked up a bivalve clamshell and squeezed it shut to make sure the shell closed tight then moved near where Alou and Frederico sat on a tule mat.

The native said a few easy going words to Alou. Banter about life in general.

Frederico watched and listened to every word Paha said. Alou didn't bother to translate. The clamshell made the boy curious and he wondered what he was going to use it for.

"Alou, what is he going to do with that clam?" Frederico asked, unable to hold his tongue any longer.

"Watch Frederico. Have you ever noticed that my father doesn't have hair on his face? If you watch him for a few minutes you'll see why," Alou answered.

To his astonishment Paha started plucking facial hairs out by the root. He used the lips of the clams as tweezers and every pull brought a grimace to Paha's face. Relatively hairless after all these years of plucking, the process took less then a minute.

Paha finished and rubbed his face to lessen the sting. Frederico's mouth opened in astonishment. Surely that hurt he thought.

Paha saw the boy looking incredulously in his direction so he reached over and plucked one of Frederico's unruly eyebrows unexpectedly. The boy was startled but unhurt. Paha started laughing and Alou joined him. Frederico loosened up when he realized they were just trying to break the ice.

For a half an hour he had been watching the native, scarcely moving or talking the whole time. Frederico's apprehension paralyzed him, hindering his natural urge to explore and tinker. Sitting still was not one of his better traits. Keeping quiet for long stretches was even less likely.

Finally, Frederico started laughing and Alou and Paha joined in. When the laughter subsided Alou stood up and retrieved some stone implements out of Paha's hut. Paha went over and placed a few more dry sticks of oak on the growing fire he had started. Normally, Paha ate breakfast much later in the morning. He worked better with an empty stomach. But today, with Alou and Frederico visiting, he agreed to eat early for the hungry boy's sake.

Alou sat a mortar and pestle on a flat surface and placed a milling rock with an acorn sized divot next to it to prepare for breakfast. In her hand she yielded a fist sized round rock. Frederico was very interested in Paha's cookware. Mortars and pestles were commonly found next to the rancho. They came in all sizes and shapes. The sandstone pestle Alou laid out was about eight inches long and had a flange on the end. Paha had painted the pestle handle red.

The mortar had been pecked with a hard, pointed flint rock. First a groove had been pecked around the top edge. Next, knobs were pecked on the top and broken off with sharp blows. The top was flattened eventually and a rim was formed. Then the inner crumbles in the bowl were removed.

Alou moved the milling stone directly in front of her and grabbed a handful of dried oak acorns from a basket. Using the round stone to crack open the nuts, she hit only hard enough to crack the shells open without mashing the nutmeat inside. When she was done Alou rubbed the broken pieces of nuts in her palms to separate the loose shells from the nutmeat. The rest of the shell was removed by throwing the basket of bits in the air. The sifting motion brought the larger pieces of the shells to the surface and these were discarded by hand. What was left was poured into a bowl of water to leach for a short time. The leftover chaff floating on the surface was poured off. She rinsed the milling stone with water then ground the damp nutmeat into flour as fine as possible.

Alou placed the wet acorn flower and half as much water into a clay pot she called an olla, then placed this pot on the fire to boil. Alou knew it would take about thirty minutes to cook. Just enough time for her to grind some juniper berries for flavoring.

Paha stoked the fire with a small piece of bark.

Frederico watched with great anticipation. Antsy, he asked Alou if he could help.

"Alou, let me help grind those berries, please," he begged. She gladly allowed him a chance.

"Here Frederico, do it like this," she instructed as she showed the boy the proper technique of grinding.

Frederico took the mortar off the platform and tried to balance it on a higher ledge of rock. In his excitement he knocked it off the ledge onto the boulders below. The mortar split in two on contact. Frederico was extremely upset with himself. How could he have been so clumsy?

Paha saw the horrified look in Frederico's eyes and patted him on the back. Alou told him,

"Don't worry, it was an accident. Paha has many others like it. Really."

Paha went into his hut and retrieved two more mortars. One was finished and he gave that to Alou to use for grinding the juniper berries. The other was half finished and he gave that one to Frederico. Then, with great patience, he showed Frederico how to finish pecking the groove across the top. He handed the stone hammer and a pointed piece of flint to the boy and motioned for him to get started. Frederico started pecking, glad to be doing something constructive after causing such a mess.

Before long the acorn gruel was done and the berries pulverized. She reached into another basket and pulled out some ball shaped pieces of honeydew. These sugary sweet morsels had been gathered by Paha in the summer and were used as sweeteners.

"What are those?" Frederico asked.

"They're the sweet droppings of aphids left on the grass during the summer. The grass was cut, threshed and winnowed and the honeydew that was leftover was made into marble sized balls. It's used primarily as a sweetener for the acorn gruel," Alou revealed.

Alou put all the acorn gruel in three different wooden bowls and added several balls of honeydew and some pulverized juniper berries.

"Time to eat," she told Paha and Frederico. Frederico stopped pecking at the half-finished mortar and sat on a tule mat. Paha sat next to the boy and Alou put the food in front of them.

"Eat it. It's very good for you. It'll make you strong," she said. All the stone pecking had built up quite an appetite in Frederico and he hungrily devoured the meal.

"Would you like something to drink, perhaps some cool water?" She offered.

"Yes Alou, I'm very thirsty. It's hard work to make a mortar," Frederico responded. Paha shook his head to signal he wanted water too.

Alou went into the hut and came out with a tall basket. She needed both arms to carry the heavy water container because of it's size. Alou removed a fibrous plug from the neck of the basket and poured separate cups of water.

Frederico had a puzzled look on his face.

"Alou, how can a basket hold water?"

She laughed,

"Ah, magic," she teased.

Paha said something to Alou pertaining to the boy's question and she answered that Frederico's curiosity had been piqued by the water basket.

Paha wanted to reveal the magic process, pleased Frederico was showing such an interest. He hurried to his hut and returned with a tightly coiled basket, several small stones about two inches in diameter, and a block of black asphaltum.

The basket was made of tule, split and then twisted into a two-ply cord. The narrow neck had a flared rim about three inches long and was coated with a brownish black tarry substance. Overall, the basket was nearly eighteen inches high and about ten inches in diameter. It differed from the other baskets in that it wasn't perfectly symmetrical or decorated. Paha looked very proud of his water basket. He had spent a lot of time on this one. Paha still needed to coat the inside, the outside neck, mouth, rim, and the bottom at least one more time with the melted asphaltum.

Paha's busy demonstration captivated Frederico. He was so different from anyone he had ever met. The natives who worked on the rancho originally came from the missions. Most of their old ways were a distant memory. In Paha's case he was fortunate to have lived the native way free from the shackles of modern civilization. This set him apart from the others.

Bits of the asphaltum were tossed into the basket. The hot walnut sized stones were retrieved from the fire and dropped into the mouth of the basket. Paha let the asphaltum melt before rolling the basket in a clockwise direction. He kept rolling, adding more asphaltum and hot rocks as needed and finally succeeded in coating the interior with the gooey substance. The leftover tarry liquid was spread around the neck and smeared on the bottom. Then, Paha set the basket on a flat stone and filled it with water. He took the extra step of putting water on the flat stone to cool it.

"He has to fill it and rinse it for three days before it's ready," Alou added.

Frederico was amazed. Already today he had witnessed the morning rituals of a proud native, eaten breakfast with him, drank cool water from his waterproof basket, and learned to peck a mortar. What a great way to start the day.

Alou realized it was getting late and told her father they must be going. He understood and even gave Frederico a pinch to assure him he was a real living native and not some figment of his imagination. The boy reached over and gave the native a pinch back. Pinch buddies. They all had a long laugh over that one.

Alou and Frederico said their good-byes and left. They walked a different path back to their horses, taking great pains not to leave a trail.

On the way home Frederico couldn't help but feel as though his life had been changed. He was thrilled with the day's experience and filled with great respect for Paha, the sole remaining native man living life the traditional way. Alou was happy for the both of them, Paha, her father, who needed respect and Frederico the boy, who had more pressing needs.

≈ 10 ≈

A couple of days later Alou caught up to Frederico in his room, eager to share her joy. She remembered the delight in Frederico's eyes when he had met her father for the first time. The sparkle still twinkled. What a positive difference it had made in the boy.

"Frederico, my father likes you. He thinks you're a wonderful boy and would like to meet with us today. There are some things he would like to show you. Your curiosity is very encouraging to my father. He's never seen that degree of enthusiasm before. Paha is a wise man and he sees something in you that stirs his spirit and gives him reason to live. When they took me to the missions no one was left. Our knowledge as a people had been passed down to the children over thousands of years. There were no more children. The chain had never been broken until now. With no suitable young men to tutor my father thought that his link was the last. This saddened him and eventually took away his pep. The spirits had not answered his prayers until now. Frederico, we need to embrace this man's spirit. Give him his due. His life has been one of great power and honor yet no one had witnessed it. Those long years of isolation have left his spirit lonely. Before he passes, I know he would like to share some of his life. Perhaps you'll understand later when your own soul is searching for realization. You must trust in me, you are doing my father a great service and a big favor with your enthusiasm. Please don't underestimate the power of your actions."

Frederico was elated with her wonderful wisdom. She answered a pressing question and plucked that feather of doubt concerning Paha's intentions. Frederico sensed his acceptance but was unsure until now. Alou's uplifting, encouraging speech of mutual respect and admiration brought great pleasure to the boy's youthful soul.

Frederico's short life had already experienced many more downturns then good fortunes. Loved and coddled, surrounded by friends and family, Frederico's early life was a slice of paradise. His mother was around even though the troubled signs were starting. His father, a wealthy, successful businessman, had used underlings to run the day-to-day operations, leaving him plenty of time to play with all his kids, including Frederico. His father read him books, taught him to read, and told him wonderful stories about his days as a merchant sea captain. Everything changed at once for the boy. Their family moved to the rancho, his mother immediately took ill, and his father became totally preoccupied with the much more difficult rancho business. The first two years had been incredibly difficult for the whole family. The brothers he had played with so peacefully in Santa Barbara had turned into virtual terrors of intimidation. With no real supervision, the twins were free to roam and destroy without consequence. Things were pretty bleak for Frederico.

The simple fact that Paha liked him and wanted to spend time with him lifted his spirits to new heights.

"Alou, let me tell you from the bottom of my heart that I will never turn from your father. He gives me reason to live. My heart is happy again. When does he want to meet? Let's go now. I want to see him," Frederico said sincerely.

It was rather late in the morning to slip away unnoticed but Frederico insisted.

"I want to go today for an hour or two. That'll be enough. Come on, let's go."

"Okay, if you insist," she laughed.

Frederico met Alou a short distance up the trail. They hurried excitedly to Paha's hut. As before they took another route in. Paha heard them coming and was waiting near the front of his tule hut. Both man and boy smiled warmly when they saw each other. The old native held out his fingers and Frederico did the same. Their odd finger shake was unique to their friendship.

Paha said some kind words to Alou and she reciprocated. After a short discussion between the two Alou turned to Frederico and said,

"My father noticed your great admiration for ordinary native things. He thinks you might like to see some of his treasures. This is a very special offer. Some of his treasures are exceptionally valuable and full of supernatural powers."

Those last two words perked up Frederico's ears. When Alou told him Paha was a shaman the young boy's mind overflowed with wonder. For years the rancho natives talked of the great and powerful men who were shamans. Their powers were legendary and steeped in the supernatural.

Paha motioned for them to sit on the tule mats he had provided while Alou explained his serious manner.

"These objects have significant meaning to Paha. We must respect his reverence."

Frederico watched, filled with anticipation of the treasure show to follow. Paha cleared his throat and said something to Alou then went into the hut and returned with a fantastic topknot headdress adorning his proud head. The headdress was studded with long owl feathers tied in bunches and the down cord skirt he wore had feathers interwoven on fiber cords that hung from a braided waistband. Wing feathers of the great horned owl adorned the hemline, adding a special designer touch. Paha looked splendid as he paraded back and forth striking various poses. At one point he dashed into his hut and came out with a three and a half foot long self-bow. One arrow was nocked and another held under his arm. He stepped forward imitating his stealth mode. Paha made a hoofing noise like a deer and fired his arrow into a deer sized bush. It found the mark and he let out a loud whoop. Then he turned and did a victory dance.

Frederico was absolutely thrilled. He stood up and started clapping and hooting his own song and dance. Alou and Paha laughed and joined in the boy's impromptu shimmy.

Great gobs of joy flowed between the three of them. Inspired, Paha struck one last pose then retreated into his hut. In a few minutes he emerged minus the topknot headdress but still wearing his ceremonial down cord skirt. In his hands he held one of the most intricately decorated baskets the boy had ever seen. With a great deal of respect he announced the nature of his treasures.

Paha sang a native song in honor of the moment, minus the melody, and a bit on the croaky side. The serious nature in which it was done convinced Frederico that whatever was concealed in the basket had great significance.

Paha's trinket basket was globular in shape and had a slightly narrow lid. He took the lid off and pulled out an intricately inlaid wooden bowl close to five inches in diameter. Alou quietly commented on the origin. She remembered her father making that bowl many years ago.

"My father made this as a gift for a brave native man who had helped my father in tough times. Before he could give it to him, however, the friend was killed in the revolt at La Purisima Mission. He was my father's best friend so Paha kept this carved wooden oak bowl as a reminder of their good times together."

Paha held it out and gave it to Frederico to hold. The boy cradled the precious bowl. Perfectly formed and polished it appeared to be sealed with a red greasy paint. The surface gleamed in the afternoon sun. Along the rim, Paha had inlaid a line of shell beads. Their perfect spacing and consistent size had great aesthetic appeal. The finely carved bowl reminded Frederico more of an art piece then as a bowl for everyday use. Paha obviously placed a great deal of sentimental value on this. The beauty of the piece moved the boy, nearly bringing him to tears as he thought how sad Paha must've been to lose his best friend.

Frederico had also lost his best friend but not to soldier's bullets. He felt a common bond with Paha in their shared loss of friendships. Very gently he handed it back to Paha and thanked him in Spanish.

"Thank you Paha. My condolences to you on losing your best friend," Frederico relayed through Alou. The native man looked surprised and honored. Frederico's heartfelt plea impressed Paha. The native said something gentle and kind to his daughter in response. Alou was visibly pleased to hear what he said.

"Frederico, my father wants to know if you'd like to make one of these wooden bowls. You could settle some of your inner turmoil this way. My father finds making things very therapeutic. This is one way he has stayed sane all these years. He wants to show you how to do it. You must be patient because it will take time," Alou reminded.

Once again Frederico felt honored. Of course he would like to learn this special skill. The boy told her,

"Alou, tell your father I'm honored by his offer and that I cherish our time together."

"Some other day we'll begin," Alou told the eager student, adding,

"My father has some more things to show you. Items with special supernatural significance."

What could those be Frederico wondered? He could barely wait to see.

Paha reached into his trinket basket and pulled out a small, carved figure of a killer whale. Called 'Caxnipaxat' by the old natives, he obviously held this animal in the highest esteem. Paha looked hard at this personal talisman. Carved from steatite and polished to a high gloss, the black whale figure had shell beads inlaid around the tall dorsal fin and two more that looked like eyes imbedded in the head.

Alou said something to Paha who hesitated a second before shaking his head.

"Frederico, my father carved this whale effigy many years ago. He took special care to make a mouth and a blowhole because he wanted the whale to be as realistic as possible. When my father was young he was inspired by a spectacular display of power by one of these sea animals.

Before I was born, my father and the rest of the village men used to go to the rocky reefs near Cave Landing. At certain times of the year hundreds of seals and sea lions lounged on top of several large rocks along the beach.

Offshore, during the gray whale migration, numerous killer whales lurk below the surface to pick off wounded, sick, or young whale calves. On occasion hungry killer whales would rush seals swimming in the water, scaring the panicked seals onto the sandy shore. The native men knew the seals would be preoccupied trying to avoid the killer whales. At the most opportune moment men would rush from behind rocks and club the seals as they dashed back into the ocean.

My father participated in this harvest many times. On one special day a killer whale came charging in, scaring dozens of flapping seals out of the water. In the rush to devour a seal the mighty sea beast beached himself momentarily between sets of waves. When my father stepped out from behind his hiding place he stood less then ten feet from the killer whale.

Staring eye to eye, my father told me that in those precious few seconds the killer whale talked to him. He warned Paha of the danger his village would face someday. Something supernatural passed between them, linking them in spirit. Paha realized he had just met his first personal spirit guide. That day was etched in my father's heart and soul forever. Some of the other men witnessed the exchange of power and were awestruck. When they returned to the village with meat and blubber word passed quickly of Paha's encounter with the killer whale. Our chief took my father aside and questioned him at length about his fantastic ordeal. Satisfied with the authenticity of the spirit contact, the chief declared my father a shaman of great power and made him the village Paha or master of ceremonies. From that day on my father's name was changed to Paha. Travelers from distant villages heard about my father and made time to meet with him. Wisdom was passed to him from shamans of great importance. At one point, my father was declared a man of power by the combined villages of all our tribes. Thousands knew his name and looked up to him. Those were my father's glory years. After the soldiers took us, my father stayed at the village, vowing never to surrender. With his special powers there was no doubt he could survive alone. Paha used his powers wisely, without influence and his spirits sustained him for forty years," Alou finished.

Paha looked shy, almost distant, during Alou's story. He had only allowed Alou to recite their family legend because he felt the boy needed to know such power existed.

"Frederico, you must accept the fact that supernatural forces play a major part of our daily lives. If you believe this you can find your own personal spirit guide and use it to resolve some of life's biggest conflicts."

Frederico was speechless. He had never heard such an incredible story. The boy didn't know how to respond. Suddenly, something shook the boy.

Alou saw Frederico's face flush then go pale really quickly. She crouched next to the boy, ready to catch him if he fainted. Frederico was momentarily unsteady, overcome with a powerful sense of being.

"My heart felt like it stopped beating," Frederico whispered.

Alou heard this and turned to Paha who was nodding his

head knowingly, certain he had just witnessed the rebirth of a powerful force. In a tribute to the spirits he sang a special singsong over and over.

Frederico's color returned and within seconds he regained his balance. The boy saw that Paha and Alou were talking animatedly about the significance of this event. From time to time they would look at Frederico and express murmurs of astonishment.

Alou turned to Frederico and said,

"Frederico, Paha told me he saw a bright spirit force enter you and take residence within your soul. He believes you have been anointed by a powerful spirit entity in the upper world to carry forth the ways of our people. This is the sign he has been waiting for. He saw the change in you and now your aura shines forth like the sun. He is honored to have been a witness to this."

Alou continued,

"He also told me there isn't a lot of time left for him to teach you our ways and it's imperative he enlighten you very soon. I promised my complete cooperation."

Frederico stumbled back a few feet, totally confused about his new role. The powers that sparked such curiosity in the boy were opening doors and asking him to come in. Although he felt different the boy couldn't explain how.

"But Alou, I have no answers," he mumbled.

"Don't worry Frederico, your spirit will guide you and help when the time is right. You have been anointed to carry a special message to the newcomers. Hold your head high and feel the energy," Alou suggested.

Frederico was bowled over. It sounded so true he decided to accept it and attempt to understand more as he gained knowledge.

"One more thing Frederico. Paha has something for you," Alou said excitedly.

Paha dug deep in his trinket basket and pulled out a black raven effigy. Shell beads marked the eyes and tail feathers of the carved figure. It was small, no more then three inches high.

Paha put the dark raven into the bewildered boy's hands and gingerly closed Frederico's fingers around the bird figure. Paha mouthed some ancient words of wisdom, smiled his crooked grin, and released his hold.

Frederico opened his hand, took a look at the effigy and gasped,

"Thank you," to the native man.

Paha entered his hut and placed his trinket basket in a special hiding place. Before he did this he took out several special items and wrapped them in a tule mat. Without saying goodbye Paha left Alou and Frederico.

"My father needs help with this big teaching job. There are secrets he knows that can ease this task. He has gone off to a special place to prepare and will signal me when the time is right," she said.

"We better go now while the sun still shines. No one must know of this Frederico. The sacred ways of our tribe are at stake," Alou related.

"Alou, what is this? Will this figurine help me? I don't understand," Frederico commiserated.

"Please tell me what this is all about," Frederico pleaded.

"Frederico, that is the effigy of a raven. My father once told me he kept the personal effigy of a great and powerful man who had given it to him with the understanding that he pass it to the next rightful owner. He was extremely protective of this effigy and as far as I know, you are the only person besides myself to ever see it. This great, wise shaman told my father of the enormous supernatural power represented by the raven. This knowledge is only for the rightful owner of this effigy and you will be enlightened to the meaning of all this not a minute too soon. Hold it tight when you carry it with you. Don't let anyone ever take it, especially Miguel. This is serious business Frederico. Please remember this and respect it," Alou told him.

"I will Alou. Paha would never have given me this without good reason. I will keep this with me everywhere I go. I noticed there was a hole drilled in it. I think I'll put a string through it and hang it around my neck, close to my heart," Frederico determined.

Alou agreed and they made a hasty retreat back home, exhilarated by the spirit of Frederico's transformation.

≈ 11 ≈

Frederico fell ill with the flue after his meeting with
Paha and Alou. The boy was bedridden for a full week.
During his sickness the boy experienced a series of strange,
bewildering dreams dealing with the supernatural. His role
remained unknown in the vivid ordeal.

When he felt well enough to ride again Frederico
talked Alou into taking him for a short visit with Paha. Alou
was eager to comply. Paha had been signaling his desire to
meet for days. Alou and the boy rode out together under
darkening, stormy skies. In the distance large curtains of
rainy downpours pounded the rough, gray sea. Localized
rain conditions varied widely between torrential rainstorms
and eerie calm.

Paha was not at the meeting spot. Alou waited for a
while but he didn't show. Concerned, she set out for his tule
hut.

"Paha, father, where are you?" She called from outside

the hut. Inside there was a stirring noise but no answer.

"Paha, are you in there?" Alou summoned nervously.

"Alou, is that you?" Paha called mournfully from inside. She immediately entered the hut and left Frederico outside waiting.

Alou found her father wrapped in a large bearskin. He was weeping into his hands as his body shuddered with an immense emotional pain.

"Paha, what's wrong?" She cried. Dropping to his side she curled up next to him. Paha told her he grieved for his lost wife and confessed that the pain of her horrible death incapacitated him. He wept too for the missed chances to be with Alou as her everyday father. The soldiers of the mission took all that from him almost forty years ago and the memory still haunted him. Sometimes, he told her, he could feel his wife breathing next to him in the middle of the night and could hear her sigh. When he reached out for her she was not there. This trick of the sky people confused him, leaving him very sad. That was why he mourned. He missed her and wanted to be with her soon.

All the knowledge of a hundred shamans could not help Paha. He was angry and ashamed. The soldiers could hardly be blamed because they were only puppets of an evil empire. The dark malevolent beings from the lower world were involved somehow. He had every reason to believe they had risen up one night and corrupted the spiritual minds of the padres.

Alou was deeply moved. The mother she lost at ten was hard to remember. From what she could recall her mother was a fine, gracious, loving woman who had a soft spot in her soul for everyone around her. The oppressive times that followed her death obliterated most of Alou's native memory.

Frederico was getting anxious. He was alarmed by the sound of crying inside the hut. He feared something terrible had happened.

"Alou, Alou, are you okay?" He yelled,

"Is Paha with you? What's wrong?" Frederico cried, emotionally upset.

Alou emerged a few seconds later and told Frederico,

"We must go. My father has some very important issues to take care of."

Alou tried to slide by Frederico but he wouldn't let her until she answered his question.

"No, Alou, what's happened to Paha? Is he dying?" Frederico asked hoarsely.

"Oh no my little one. If you must know, Paha grieves for my mother and his wife. It was at this time of the year when the soldiers came and took me, killing my mother in the process. All these years have not healed his painful wounds. They fester constantly," Alou explained sadly.

"Let's go Frederico. Paha needs time to mourn alone. There's someplace he needs to go. My mother is buried very close to here in our old village cemetery. This sacred site has eluded discovery and her grave site remains pristine. Paha has maintained the site, dedicating himself to her spirit. That is where he goes in his times of need, to recharge his will and seek solace from the past."

Alou didn't say goodbye to her father as she hustled the boy away. Paha had asked her to not let the boy see him in that condition. He was afraid he might scare the boy and hoped her young charge would understand.

Frederico rode home completely deflated. His eagerness to learn from Paha had been stymied. Frederico had the heart of a twelve year old and it bruised easily at such a tender age. Confused the boy wondered if all the things Paha had told him still held true. Frederico kept his faith standing strong in the face of adversity.

Remarkably, Miguel and Carlos took a brief respite from their taunting and teasing. Frederico knew this would not last for long. Sooner or later they would erupt, burning him with their lava tongues and bombastic sarcasm.

Back at his hut Paha rose from his bed and threw a large deerskin cape over his shoulders. He would be spending the night in the cemetery lying by her grave. Neither the approaching rain or the cold of the night would keep him from his annual sojourn. He placed his necessities in a large knotted carrying net and set out for the sacred cemetery.

The rain started as Paha ascended the small plateau. Big wet, cold, dreary drops. Several years ago Paha had constructed a small rain shelter, purposely keeping it primitive and disguised from intruders eyes. Used only by him in the lowest of times.

Set in a hollow at the base of a cliff, a big oak and smaller willows shielding it from the wind and the rain. Carefully placed tules on the floor inside provided a small degree of dry comfort. This would be his Spartan home for the night as it had been before during countless nights of despair.

Darkness approached as the rain came down in buckets. Inside, no water made it to where Paha lay. Just in case an extra layer of rabbit pelts lay heaped head to toe over the native. From his prone position he had a direct view of his wife's grave. Here he would stay as a protective sentry for all the departed souls.

The cemetery was a sacred place. A suitable high

plateau, usually close to the village, was chosen and sometimes surrounded by a wood fence. No fence marked Paha's cemetery, however. That would have been too risky. Instead, a large stone marker identified it as a sacred site.

His wife's grave was marked with a wooden pole almost eight feet tall and also by a wooden plank painted in a black and white checkerboard design. He tended to her grave frequently keeping it free of weeds and debris. The other graves scattered around hers were mostly chiefs and important people. Paha maintained those as well as an offering of faith to the resident spirits. These powerful men had elaborate graves decorated with whale rib bones and carved, painted stone slabs. Their native cemetery occupied more then two acres. Less important graves had no decorations but were far more numerous.

Inside the shelter Paha remembered the good days of his life and gave thanks for the long life he had led. He wondered aloud if these days were his last. Old age had made his bones brittle and someday the challenges of his life would be too severe to overcome.

For now the warm overlapping blankets heated his tired body. Paha slipped into a deep slumber and waited for the dream world to surround him. Sometimes in this dream his dead wife came to him and became one with his soul. He never wanted to leave her embrace.

Rain pounded the site all night. A small family of field mice took refuge inside, sharing the shelter in complete harmony with Paha.

Far away on the rancho Frederico slipped under his heavy wool blankets and prayed hard for another chance to learn from Paha. Their time together had been wonderful. The best of his young life and Frederico yearned for more.

At the most important juncture in his life Frederico prayed for a happy ending.

≋ 12 ≋

      Several days later Alou took Frederico to visit Paha. She couldn't stay so she left the boy, promising to come back later to accompany him home.

      Frederico was nervous. This was the first time he'd been alone with Paha. Without Alou's interpretation how would he know what Paha was saying? She said Paha wouldn't have a problem communicating with him and she was sure that Paha could entertain the boy. Native ways were incredibly varied. Their mundane activities became a rip-roaring adventure for Frederico. If nothing else Paha knew he could prepare him a snack.

      Today, Paha had made plans to take Frederico on a rabbit hunt. Conditions favored the bow and arrow. Paha used other methods, including the rabbit stick and snare traps, but those methods took more time and patience to learn. The native wanted to teach the boy about conserving food.

      Inside the hut Paha dug for his favorite self-bow,

Frederico waited patiently outside sitting on his favorite tule mat. The flaps of the hut opened and out walked Paha with his bow and arrows. Frederico's uneasiness was soon relieved by the native's good-natured antics. Paha, a natural born comedian, kept the boy in stitches as he impersonated a great hunter. With great fanfare Paha mimicked the prancing and hopping motions of today's prey, the rabbit. His antics revealed to Frederico that they were going rabbit hunting and judging by the bow in his hands, were going to use arrows.

The native came close to Frederico and showed him the bow. The staff of elderberry measured four and a half feet long and about one and a half inches in diameter. Paha had already strung the bow with a long piece of two-ply deer sinew. Usually he kept this bow unstrung until right before the hunt.

For small game such as rabbits Paha like to use self-arrows of toyon wood fletched with feathers and sharpened in a fire. The end of the shaft had a little v-groove to nock the string.

Frederico was surprised the arrows didn't all have chert arrowheads. Didn't all arrows have a stone tip? He didn't know those kinds of arrows were only used for large game with the much stronger sinew backed bow.

There were perhaps a dozen toyon arrows in Paha's deerskin quiver. None had arrowheads and a few were featherless shoots of sagebrush.

Frederico was very excited about the hunt. There were lots of brush rabbits along the edge of the dunes. They scampered everywhere in the morning, stopping occasionally to nibble on tender grass shoots. Frederico figured it would be a snap to shoot a few.

Instead of heading out right away Paha insisted on

practicing a bit. Situated around the edge of the clearing several small rabbit sized bushes grew low to the ground. Paha pointed his fingers at the low bushes and did a few hop hops. Then, in a slow deliberate manner, he stalked the bush, edging closer with an arrow attached to the string.

In short measured movements Paha drew back the shaft, holding it with his middle and index fingers. When he let the arrow go it flew straight and fast scoring a direct hit on the faux rabbit bush.

Under his armpit he had another arrow. This time he ran to the other side of the clearing while nocking an arrow on the run. It was a clever demonstration of his hunting prowess. This arrow also struck the target bush dead center. Paha smiled and motioned for the boy to try.

Frederico stood and took the bow and a single arrow from Paha. Very deliberately Paha made the motion of pulling the arrow back and releasing it. Confident the boy understood he placed Frederico's fingers on the arrow and the string, holding them there for a long second to ingrain the proper position. Frederico pulled the arrow as far back as he could to show Paha he could do it. A short distance away the old native evaluated his style. He made a slight adjustment in how the boy held the bow, going from almost vertical to nearly horizontal. This way the arrow rested on top of the bow beam and was held in place by the boy's left index finger. It was not exactly the way Paha did it but it suited the boy's smaller arms and hands.

A few yards in front of him a small grassy shrub sprouted from the sandy terrain. Paha pointed to the bush and motioned for him to try and hit it with the arrow.

Frederico pulled the arrow back like he was taught and sighted down the shaft towards the target. It looked right on so he released the string and the arrow went flying. The shaft zipped from the bow and flew directly over the bush, sticking in the sand about a foot high.

Paha motioned for him to try again. He reached into his quiver and handed the boy another arrow. Frederico took aim and shot it a bit lower. This time the arrow struck the top of the small target and flew right through it.

He took another arrow from Paha, determined to get it right this time. He aimed at the bush again but this time even lower. True to his new aim the arrow found the middle of the bush, burying itself half way in.

Frederico did a funny shimmy shake and whooped it up. The boy's celebratory spirit tickled the old native and he joined Frederico in his impromptu victory dance.

Paha was genuinely relieved to see the stress in the boy melt away. A newfound sense of adventure had filled the boy's heart and the old native basked in its glow.

Paha went and retrieved the arrows. He placed them in his deerskin quiver and glanced at the boy as if to say, ready for the real thing?

Together they walked a short distance to a small clearing where sagebrush peppered the landscape.

Paha held his finger to his mouth, nocked an arrow and started slowly moving forward. His eyes were wide open and his ears seemed to be tuned to every sound when something caught his attention out of the corner of his eye.

Without a seconds hesitation Paha drew the bow back and let the arrow fly. A large brush rabbit, almost completely hidden behind a leafy branch, took the full force of the arrow directly in the shoulder. The shaft penetrated the animal, impaling him against the firm earth. The rabbits back legs kicked frantically for a few seconds before stopping.

Paha skipped the whoop. With his hands to his lips he moved slowly to Frederico and handed him the bow and one arrow. The native nudged him forward and pointed to the same general area where he had shot the first rabbit.

Frederico walked towards the bushes and inadvertently stepped on a dry branch, cracking it. More then one rabbit sprinted away in terror.

"Ahhh!" Frederico mouthed, frustrated at his lack of stealth. He turned to Paha who was pointing frantically at another small bush to the side of where the boy stood.

Frederico saw where he was pointing and was able to identify the short stubby ears of a small brush rabbit. This took Frederico completely by surprise. He thought all the rabbits had escaped. With his heart beating a million miles an hour he pulled the arrow back and sighted down the shaft, aiming a tad low. Almost automatically he released the arrow. It flew straight at the rabbit and penetrated right through its chest. The rabbit struggled briefly then relaxed, free from the rigors of life.

Frederico expected a big dose of pride but felt bad instead. The brush rabbit was dead and the harsh facts of subsistent hunting saddened him. When he looked at Paha, however, he saw a look of joy. The native ran over and picked up Frederico's rabbit, holding it up by its back legs. This gift of nature would sustain Paha for another day and that was good.

They walked to the hut grateful for the bounty of nature. On the way Frederico noticed one large ragged scar on Paha's right shoulder. The old native saw him looking at his disfigurement and decided to have some fun with it. Paha picked up the pace then turned and rolled into a grand act of pantomime.

Paha held his bow high with his chest puffed up with pride and waved the long bow around. Suddenly he yelled a strong challenge to an unseen enemy. Paha stood, feet squarely planted beneath him and offered his body up as a target.

Frederico thought Paha had lost his mind. What was he doing? He seemed to be taunting some imaginary opponent. The native took an arrow from his quiver and held it out at arms length then brought it back to him, pantomiming the flight of an incoming arrow. In slow motion the imaginary incoming arrow hit him exactly on the scar on his shoulder. He tucked the arrow playfully under his arm and staggered back, letting out a groan. Paha fell to one knee, dramatically over hyped his arrow injury, then lay still on the ground for a second with his eyes closed.

Frederico gasped, certain his native friend had suffered some kind of serious injury. He ran over to where he lay.

"Paha, Paha, Say something!" He cried in a fit of panic. The foxy native opened one of his eyes to see if the rancho boy was close enough then grunted real loud. This startled Frederico. Paha burst out in the longest, hardest laugh the boy had ever heard. The whole dramatic act confused him. Without Alou to explain he could only imagine the story behind it.

Frederico laughed nervously, slightly bewildered by Paha's antics. Paha kept on laughing, amused to have tricked Frederico. Pretty soon Frederico began to realize he had been had and loosened up. Together they giggled about it all the way back to the hut.

Paha took the rabbits from his fiber cord belt and prepared them for cooking. First he cleaned the entrails from the body cavity and peeled off the skins, saving them for later. He planned on making another blanket before the nippy winter arrived.

In the area he used for cooking Paha set out to make a fire. Frederico watched intently as the grizzled veteran of the wilds retrieved his fire making tools and sat down beside the boy.

The one thing about the natives that fascinated Frederico more then anything else was their magical ability to start fires. This skill had escaped Frederico's understanding earlier and he longed for a demonstration.

On the rancho, coals from the previous day's fire were used to start the next. When the need did arise to start a new fire, flint sticks were used with less then perfect efficiency. The newcomers were not privy to the native ways and their subtle choice of tinder. Paha's woodpile was consistently upgraded for quality. Wet wood was laid out to dry and the more suitable dry branches were used first.

Paha's fire making kit consisted of a drill stick of guatomote about a foot long and 1/4 inch in diameter. The hearth, less then eight inches long and 3/4 inch wide, was made of coastal sagebrush and had several small holes drilled near the edge. The sides had v-shaped notches adjacent to the edges of the holes. Paha's basic fire drill had been used by his people for thousands of years and worked well.

Paha had made this fire drill long ago. The socket was no more then a 1/4 inch deep and specifically angled to provide the greatest amount of fiction. The tip was blunt to take advantage of it.

Paha spun the drill stick between his palms in the bored out socket. He went up and down the shaft again and again with his busy hands. The stored heat in the wood powder worked its way into the groove next to the notch. Soon a glowing ember started and was carefully blown on by Paha until the tinder ignited.

Paha was very proficient in making fires. He knew how to use his strength and coordination to maintain the required pressure in a continuous fashion. Paha used dry shredded sagebrush as tinder and the dry bark of the red oak for a good hot fire.

The cleaned rabbits were skewered with a stick and stuck into the ground so that the carcasses were directly above the searing flames. Every so often Paha would twist the broiling meat around so that both sides cooked.

Something about the fire drew the two closer. The flickering flames and sizzling meat was a feast for the senses and no dialog was necessary.

When the rabbits looked cooked enough Paha removed them from the sticks and placed them in a flat wooden bowl. Small bits of herbs were sprinkled on top and allowed to sit while the meat simmered.

By now Frederico was really hungry and the meat smelled delicious. He expected to strip the shreds of meat clinging to the back legs, enjoying the tasty morsel right away but Paha stopped him before he could pick the meat off the bones. The native put his hand up signaling for Frederico to wait. The boy was anxiously awaiting the first taste of his rabbit and this tested his hungry patience.

Frederico watched as Paha produced a milling stone and a round rock hammer. What was he going to do he wondered. There were no seeds or berries to grind only the cooked rabbits.

Paha cleaned off the stone slab with his hand and placed the cooked rabbit carcasses side by side on top of it. Using the hand sized rock he began pounding the rabbits, bones and all. His blows were not too hard only firm enough to break the bones. Eventually, after repeated blows, the meat and bones of the rabbit were pulverized. As he continued to tenderize the meat the mash coalesced into a homogenized lump.

Paha stopped occasionally to pick out flakes of bone too large to completely smash. This he did several times. After a few minutes he took the mass of food and folded it over. Then he smashed it some more.

Finally, both rabbits were completely processed. The meat cakes were much larger then what the pure strips of meat would have amounted to. Magically, the volume of food had been multiplied by the extra pounding. Now there was enough food for the both of them.

Paha finished pounding and picked off a few warm pieces of meat with his fingers. He carefully inspected the pulp for any hazardous bone flakes. Finding none he turned to Frederico and made a hand gesture signaling it was time to eat. He poured some cool, clear water out of his water basket and divided the rabbits in half. Served on a flat, plate sized rock the rabbit was an unrecognizable mass but smelled delicious.

Frederico took a small piece and tasted it first.

"Ummm!" He remarked as he devoured the rest, adding,

"It's good."

Frederico felt good knowing how to stretch sparse morsels of food. He was beginning to understand how native ways made use of all of nature's bounty. Never wasting anything, always conserving for later days.

Paha and Frederico finished their lunch and washed it down with long swigs of water. They cleaned off their flat stone plates and sat on tule mats recalling the hunt of the morning. Frederico kept thinking about how wonderful it was to be with Paha. There was so much to learn and it was fun too. After resting for a while in the shade Frederico realized it was time to go. He thanked Paha in Spanish, who smiled from ear to ear.

At the edge of the dunes Alou waited for her young charge. Frederico met her there and she could tell he was very happy.

"Frederico, you look so happy, did you shoot a rabbit?" She asked, clued in by the big smile on his face.

"Yes Alou. I had the best time. Your father is such a skilled hunter. One lesson from him and now I'm an expert with the bow too. He showed me how to shoot straight and true. It's easy, " Frederico boasted.

"We cooked the rabbits, smashed them with a rock and ate everything, bones and all. Paha also showed me how to make a fire. It looks hard. Your father was sweating by the time he started it. There was only one thing that puzzled me. On the way home he saw me looking at the big scar on his shoulder and started into some fantastic demonstration. From what I could gather an arrow had pierced his shoulder and caused a scar. I was horrified but your father made a big joke about it and made me laugh. What happened to him?" Frederico asked.

Alou raised her eyes and laughed,

"Oh brother, not the mock battle tale. Long ago my father suffered this injury during a mock battle. These battles were fought to settle disputes between neighboring villages. First a challenge would be issued then a time and place set for the confrontation. The participants would show up with all their war gear on. A man from one village would step forward and shoot several arrows at the opposing village man. Then an opposing member of the other side would do the same. When someone was killed or injured the mock battle was stopped and the winner declared.

My father took an arrow to the shoulder during one of those battles. Thank goodness he wasn't killed. To this day he proudly wears his scar like a badge of courage."

Frederico was thrilled by Paha's bravery. From what he knew so far about the old native this completely fit his character.

"I'm so thankful for all that's happened," Frederico remarked, adding,

"My whole life has changed for the better."

They rode for a while before Alou spoke.

"By the way, Paha wants to take you fishing with him next week," Alou revealed.

This didn't surprise Frederico. Paha was more then just a teacher, he was a friend. Alou and Frederico ventured home pleased with the way things were going.

≈ 13 ≈

On the planned fishing day Alou was called by the Captain to act as an interpreter to settle a dispute between one of the rancho men and a native servant. The rancho man, with highly suspicious motives, had accused the native servant of stealing his leather saddlebags. Supposedly, he had found them in the confines of the man's quarters but didn't actually see the man take them. The native wanted to explain his side but needed Alou to interpret. The Captain wanted to avoid a potential confrontation and he knew he could trust Alou to settle the problem.

"Frederico, I can't go with you today to see my father. My services are needed here. Pepito has accused one of the native men of stealing. He's pretty upset and wants to extract some justice but my native friend says he's innocent. It's a long story and I will tell you about it later. If I can help him avoid a beating I'll consider it a blessing from the spirits. You understand, don't you? Why don't you go alone? You know the way. Be careful. Take a different way in. Paha will be glad to see you. Go quickly, before something else comes up," she recommended.

Frederico slipped out of the rancho compound and rode to Paha's hut. He tied up his horse some distance away and walked the rest of the way.

Not far from Paha's hut a small freshwater lake sported a misty veil of fog that hung low on the water. Most of the lake was obscured. The thick stands of tule that grew along the shore were broken in places, allowing unfettered access to the lake's rim.

Frederico was milling around outside Paha's tule hut, not quite sure where he was.

"Paha, Paha, are you home?" He called out in Spanish. Not a word came from within. He hoped he hadn't forgotten about their fishing trip.

Over the sea breeze he heard a paddle splashing in the distance and went over to investigate. Out a ways the fog lifted and Frederico saw the source of the splashing. It was Paha in a tule canoe. The native saw Frederico and paddled over to shore, greeting Frederico with a hug and a fingertip shake. Paha pointed to his canoe and motioned for the boy to get in. In complete confidence Frederico climbed in and sat in the back, totally in awe of the apparently waterproof craft he floated in. Paha took the front position and pushed off the edge of the bank with his long double bladed paddle. A few quick dip of the oar propelled them towards a small island in the middle of the lake.

By the looks of things the tule canoe was made of bunched tule stalks tied together with fiber cords. This same type of canoe had been in use for thousands of years. Most of the tule stalks looked ten feet long, were still green, and provided ample buoyancy. From what Frederico could see above the water line, there were three bundles of stalks on the bottom and one bundle on each side. The bundles on the bottom were longer then the sides and thicker. All the bundles were shaped to a point and tied together with fiber cord. Twisted cattail leaves, overlapped to form a rope, were used to tie the bundles together every eighteen inches. The ends of the five individual bundles were tied together for the last three feet, completing the craft.

Frederico sat on the flat-topped canoe marveling at how steady the homemade boat was. Paha had turned the ends of the tule canoe up when he tied the bunches. This helped to make it lightweight and easily maneuverable.

Paha paddled very slowly around the island until he reached his favorite place. Tule stands completely surrounded the wind sheltered cove and picturesque views of floating ducks and bass smacking the surface slid into sight.

When he ventured into the cove he stopped paddling and opened his bag of fishing gear. Today he was going to use hooks, line and sinkers to teach Frederico how the natives fished. This was something Frederico had done before on the rancho. Only Paha's equipment was different. His had been fabricated completely out of natural ingredients. The hooks were abalone shell fragments drilled through the middle and broken to give a hook shape. Paha had rounded the outside of the abalone shell and sharpened one end to a point. The other end was notched for the fiber string. Paha had lots of these. He attached four of these hooks with small leader lines to a much stronger braided line and wrapped this braided line around a foot long piece of willow. He tied a stone sinker to the line, baited all four of the hooks with earthworms, and threw the whole set up over board.

The only thing left to do now was wait. Paha and Frederico relaxed in the warm rays of the sun. The fog lifted completely, revealing bright blue skies and the mirrored surface of the lake. In the distance a few mud hens quacked and one lonely goose honked.

Paha kept watching the line, tugging it periodically to feel for fish. Frederico watched and listened to the scene unfolding around them. The tule canoe was long enough for him to lie down in. He did that, fully extending his arms and legs. Paha smiled as the boy settled into a comfortable pose and appeared on the verge of falling asleep. He let Frederico relax, not wanting to disturb his tranquil moment.

Frederico lay on his back and watched dozens of sea gulls flying over. Their long white wings and yellow beaks visible as animated specks in the wild blue yonder. The stiff wind off the sea normally started around 11:00 A.M. It could get blustery anytime after that. Frederico liked the morning stillness. He loved the way sounds carried, unencumbered by the constant swoosh of the afternoon winds.

Paha kept checking his line to make sure the bait was still attached. He only touched the bait after he had washed his hands in the cold water. Paha knew the slightest scent of a human would spook the fish. The old native and the young boy floated in the canoe for more then an hour.

Paha was beginning to get a quizzical look on his face. The conditions of the moon and the clarity of the water were perfect and he had taken the utmost care in preparing his bait. All the hooks were sharpened and the line checked for snags or tears. Everything was perfect. Why hadn't they caught any fish?

Frederico sat up from his prone position and peered

over the edge. The water was four feet deep here and you could clearly see the grassy bottom. Beneath the surface he could see schools of tiny baby minnows darting from one place to another. Occasionally a bigger fish would swim by apparently in no big hurry.

Frederico wanted to put his hand in the water but didn't, mindful of the effect it might have on the fish. From his vantage point he could see the fishing line disappear into the weeds. Three large fish with big lippy mouths hovered next to the baited hooks. They studied the wiggling worms, their thick tail fins fanning back and forth slowly. One of the fish had large dark eyes that never moved. It was hard to decide who was relaxing the most, the fish or the fisherman.

Paha's short grunt of dissatisfaction got Frederico's attention. He resumed his sitting posture as Paha took his line out of the water. The native had another spot in mind that might be better. He wasted no time moving in that direction.

Silently, Paha paddled out of the cove towards the upper end of the lake where a large creek emptied into the water. A smile appeared on Paha's face as he stroked the oar. He liked being out on the lake.

On the bank Frederico could see a family of raccoons washing their humanlike hands in the water. Their masked faces completely unconcerned with the floating raft of tules drifting towards them. Paha paddled closer until one of the bigger raccoons stood on his hind feet for a better look at the incoming raft. Suddenly, Paha's face turned sour and he shouted at the raccoons. He paddled quickly over and scared the fish eating raccoons away. It soon became apparent why Paha had become so angry. In the water near the mouth of the creek, several man-made fish traps of willow extended into the water. They belonged to Paha.

The native stopped directly over the long conical fish traps. They were made from long sticks of willow tied to a twisted branch hoop. The hoop was about two feet in diameter and the sticks tapered to an end where they were tied together with fiber cords. Asphaltum had been applied to the cords to keep them waterproof.

The raccoons had separated several of the long sticks and eaten the fish trapped within. All three of Paha's fish traps had been violated. The damage was light so Paha pulled them from the water and wrapped spare coils of cord around the sticks to repair them. A large rock with a braided three-ply fiber cord served as an anchor.

Paha took the traps into deeper water and repositioned them in the old creek channel. He dropped the anchor rock and checked their condition. Paha seemed unsatisfied with the angle and location of the traps so he took his paddle and moved them to another spot.

The lake was deep here, probably at least twelve feet. Still, Frederico could see the bottom clearly. Something in this part of the lake was stirring up the turgidity of the water. Try as he might he couldn't see what it was.

Paha motioned for the boy to do as he did. He gave Frederico the rolled leaf that held the worms and instructed him to wash his hands in the water before touching the bait. Frederico did as he was shown and replaced the limp worms that clung to the seashell hooks. With Paha's blessing he threw the hooks back into the water and took a vigilant position on the other end of the fishing line.

They drifted over that spot for at least thirty minutes without so much as a nibble. Frederico could tell this fishing trip wasn't going according to Paha's plan. That was fine with him. The sheer joy of being with his native friend was enough. Paha took the fishing pole from the boy and pulled it to see if there was any resistance. Finding nothing on the line he put the pole down and reached for his bag of goodies. This time he didn't produce another fishing item. He took out what looked like a flute.

In fact, it was an elderwood flute. Some time ago Paha had harvested a straight green elderwood stick about two feet long and placed it in a pile of embers to harden. A toyon rod with beveled edges was used to bore a hole through the pithy center. He had let it dry a couple of days before scraping the bark off the outside. Paha liked his notes high so he cut it relatively short, about fourteen inches, and formed a mouthpiece on one end. The musical notes he desired required four holes. These were burned into the flute with the hot end of a glowing stick. A few shell beads were glued to the tube with asphaltum for decoration.

Paha put the flute to the side and pulled another item out of his bag. It was a cocoon rattle. The large cocoons of a moth had been filled with pebbles through a hole that was sealed with asphaltum. Four cocoons were tied to small sticks with fiber strings and then all four tied together. The resulting rattle was easy to use, even for a small boy.

Paha gave the rattle to Frederico. The boy shook it a few times to get the feel of it and to hear the gravelly sound it produced.

The native picked up his flute and started to play. He blew into and slightly across the side of the flute mouth while his index fingers and middle finger of both hands covered the holes.

Paha, as a wise shaman, understood the meaning of music and how it could soothe the soul. Paha blew into the flute and played a catchy tune in a soft whistling tone. Frederico joined him with the rattle and they made sweet music together.

As if by magic the big bass started biting. Paha saw his fishing line draw taut so he pulled back on the line. Instantly the line took off and a heavy bass more then eighteen inches long broke the surface with the shell hook still clinging to his lips. Paha let out a whoop and before he could retrieve the line another bass swallowed the bait on another hook. In a matter of seconds two fat bass lay flapping in the tule canoe. Paha stuck a piece of cord through the gills of both and hung them in the water where they stayed alive but calm.

Instantaneously the fishing line grew taut again and started zigzagging through the water. Paha handed the stick with the line to the boy and motioned for him to wrap it up and bring it in. Frederico played it for a bit before he hauled it into the boat.

The thrill of the fight excited the boy making him laugh with glee. He lifted the fish into the canoe and pulled the hook from its mouth. Frederico was so excited he almost let the fish flap back into the lake. This bass was smaller then the other two but had plenty of fight in it. The fish struggled frantically on the stringer stick before settling into a state of suspension.

A rush of adrenaline surged through Frederico and made his face flush pink. He could barely wait to get the line back into the water. On and on it went. After a half an hour of nonstop action the bite stopped as suddenly as it had begun. They had enough fish so he retrieved his fishing line, wrapped it around the willow stick, put his flute and rattles back in his deerskin pouch and stored them away.

The native paddled back to his launching site and,

with Frederico's help, drug the tule canoe onto the shore. They were both hungry so Paha prepared one of the bass for immediate consumption.

The native threw a few more pieces of oak bark on his smoldering fire, and with the help of a wide tule fan, quickly coaxed the fire to burn hot. The oak bark caught fire and produced perfect coals for roasting. Two fresh fish were thrown whole on the coals and broiled to perfection.

Paha and Frederico ate the flesh directly off the fish, pulling long flaky strips with their fingers. They devoured the fish quickly leaving only the bones and charred skin behind.

After resting for a minute Paha set about preparing the other bass for curing in his smoke house. Their catch today would serve him for many more meals. Frederico patted his native friend on the back and thanked him in Spanish. He knew Paha was special and vice a versa.

The long shadow cast by Paha's tule hut alerted the boy to the lateness of the day and the fact that it was time for him to go. He was accompanied a short ways by Paha who seemed unwilling to end their visit. They finally parted ways and Frederico trotted the rest of the way home on his horse. Near the rancho, his twin brothers met him unexpectedly.

"Where have you been?" Miguel bellowed.

"Yea, where did you go today?" Carlos pried obnoxiously.

Frederico kept riding, choosing to ignore their persistent questions. Unfortunately, they were not so easily put off. Miguel rode by Frederico and pushed him off his horse. The boy tumbled down somehow landing on his feet.

"You better tell us where you've been before I kick your tail," Miguel warned. Frederico remained silent. There was no way he would ever reveal the existence of Paha. No way in this world.

Miguel and Carlos kept prying while Frederico kept quiet. Finally, Miguel exploded in a fit of anger and punched his brother extremely hard in the stomach, knocking the wind out of him. Something deep inside Frederico's spirit held on, refusing to capitulate to his angry brother's demands. Surprisingly, no tears of fear overcame the boy. Some inner power or strength gave him the courage to quiet his soul.

Frustrated, the twins mounted their horses and rode off, lacing the afternoon air with strings of profanity. Frederico dusted himself off and rode home.

Alou was waiting in his room.

"I'm glad you're here Frederico, your brothers have been looking for you all day. Did you see them?" She asked.

"Yes, Alou I did. They beat me up over by the corrals but you know what, it didn't hurt that much and I would've taken a far more severe beating if necessary. There was no way I could ever give away my friend Paha. He means too much to me. I'm different now Alou. There's something deep inside of me that's indestructible."

Alou beamed with pride, saying,

"You're becoming a man Frederico. My father was right. You do have a powerful spirit and you're learning to use it wisely, without malice. You must be very grateful for this."

Frederico agreed, responding,

"Yes, my life has changed. It's better. Thank you so much for helping me. For a while I really had no interest in living. Now I see a very rosy future for myself and Paha has had a lot to do with that."

Alou gave Frederico a big hug and left him. On this special day, the boy finally began to understand the great forces at work within his soul.

≋ 14 ≋

A couple of days later Alou found Frederico in the spinning room and told him that her father would like to take him spear fishing for salmon at the river mouth.

Frederico was delirious with anticipation. A short week later, the boy rode out to meet Paha without Alou. She told him her father had specified that the boy ride out alone. This helped build the boy's character and courage according to Paha.

Alou promised to wait for him, but Frederico told her his confidence had grown to the point where he didn't really need her to accompany him anymore.

As expected Paha was waiting by his hut with a carrying net filled with miscellaneous items. He also carried an eight-foot long spear with a forked point. Made from a young fir, the one and a half inch diameter pole tapered down to a thin point. A notch was cut near the skinny end and a forked prong with barbs attached with fiber cord and asphaltum. The double-pronged spear had a number of important advantages. The two points doubled the chances a spear thruster would find the mark. Also, if both points entered the fish's body the likelihood of escape was reduced considerably. The barbs of the point made escape an even more unlikely event.

Paha, in his good-natured way, demonstrated the thrust he used. He watched Frederico out of the corner of his eye and when the boy's attention drifted for a second, he poked the boy lightly in the butt with the spear. Frederico jumped, causing Paha to laugh like crazy for a good five seconds.

The boy was slightly embarrassed but quickly regained his composure and told Paha,

"Ouch Paha. Do I look like a salmon?" Of course Paha couldn't understand him but his sarcastic remark and wide smile convinced Paha the boy enjoyed being the butt of his jokes. Their special bond grew stronger as a result. It was a medium length journey through the dunes and along the beach to get to the river mouth. Paha kept up a surprisingly quick pace. In the old days Paha would've run the whole way, running being the only mode of transportation to get somewhere fast.

Frederico was dripping with sweat by the time they reached the river. An unusually high tide had flooded the river mouth, swelling the lagoon to twice the usual size. Every few minutes, huge swells would push a large surge of water directly into the lagoon. In the frothy white foam hundreds of steelhead salmon ran the gauntlet, desperately trying to swim up river to spawn.

Paha became very excited when he saw the silvery fish dash by in a mass from the ocean into the brackish waters of the lagoon. Thousands grouped between wave sets before undertaking their annual run up the rivers and creeks of central coast California. It was an awesome sight. There were so many you could walk across the water and not get wet.

Frederico kept pointing, gasping at one big fish then doing a double take as an even bigger one swam by. Some of the big ones were over two feet long and looked like chunky torpedoes with silver scales. Paha went down to the river's edge and waded in. He planted his feet and in a swift thrust of his spear hit pay dirt. Both points had impaled a huge fish that must have weighed ten pounds. The fish thrashed around for an extended period before dying. Paha slid the fish off the spear and placed it in one of several knotted carrying nets he had brought along.

Almost casually Paha handed the long spear to Frederico and motioned for him to give it a try. The boy waded in up to his knees and readied himself for the thrust. He saw one big fish swimming by and jabbed the spear at the fish. He missed high. Again he tried, missing high for the second time. Three more times he tried and came up empty. This was a lot harder then it looked.

"Ahhh!" He groaned as he missed again.

Frederico looked over at Paha who was trying patiently to show him the correct angle of thrust. Paha held his left hand out, wiggling it to simulate a moving fish. With his right hand he thrust his pointed finger directly below the symbolic fish, demonstrating how he had to aim low to hit his mark. The refraction of the light through the water made the fish seem higher and closer then they were. Something Paha had learned as a boy.

The next time Frederico thrust the spear far lower then he would've guessed and made a direct hit on the broad shouldered fish behind the gills. Wounded, the big fish frantically flipped his powerful tail in an effort to get away. The sudden sprint almost yanked the spear from Frederico's bony hands. The boy went splashing through the water trying not to lose the spear or the fish. The native saw his exasperation and ran down the bank to where Frederico struggled with the salmon. Paha grabbed the spear near the end, close to the fish. On two they both lifted the salmon from the water and carried it to shore where Paha produced a short club and beat the fish on the head, stunning it. Another whack dispatched it. This salmon was almost twice the size of the first fish, probably closer to three feet long and twenty-five pounds in weight. It was a brute.

The two friends rested for a minute trying to catch their breath. By now Paha's carrying net was jammed with silvery fish. The native wiped some of the fish slime off his hands on a tufted bunch of filaree bush and tied his carrying net closed. He laid the spear on the ground and knelt next to the big-bodied fish. He had never seen such a stunning display of power and grace. The salmon were extraordinarily beautiful and large.

The boy lifted the sack to estimate the combined weight. It took a major effort to hoist the net. Frederico guessed it held around forty pounds of steelhead salmon.

Paha sat in the sand next to the boy and gazed into his face. Where once there was fear and depression, new joy and hope reigned. The wholesome caring nature of the boy was indescribably pure. Frederico's eyes shone like bright moons in the midnight sky and twinkled like the stars of the great Milky Way. Paha smiled, keenly aware of the great times and memories they had built together and of the good times ahead.

After that Paha's show and tell games became even

more elaborate. He took a large shark tooth out of his bag and held it up for Frederico to see. The sharp tooth was almost three inches long and captured Frederico's undivided attention. Forgetting about the fresh salmon for the moment the boy held the triangular tooth in his hands and exclaimed in Spanish,

"Wow, where did this come from?"

Paha couldn't understand his words but from the awe elicited in Frederico's squeaky voice, could tell he was greatly impressed.

Paha immediately rolled into one of his fantastic acts. He pointed to the surging sea and mimicked the actions of a huge fish. Paha chomped his jaws up and down like a great shark must have in his glory years.

Then Paha switched characters. Barking like a seal and flapping his elbows exactly the way a sea lion might, he made the swimming fish motions with his left hand and barked again like a seal as it was chasing the salmon up the river. The native imitated the seal chasing the salmon for a few seconds before turning his head and stopping. Right behind the imaginary seal he pantomimed the great white shark sneaking up on the seal with his toothy mouth chomping.

The perfectly timed response of shock brought hysterical laughter from Frederico. Paha's antics, his grand plays, were incredibly entertaining. Paha scurried about, looking back every few seconds in mock fear. Frederico was overcome by the humor of it.

The native changed characters again. He picked up the spear and started thrusting it frantically. He called to an imaginary friend who also started thrusting his spear. The ease with which Paha was able to change characters was astonishing. A third man was pantomimed thrusting his spear frantically at the giant seal-chasing shark.

Paha changed back into the great white shark, grimacing with pain each time an imaginary spear thrust found its mark. He imitated the dying death throes of the shark, signaling his death with a pronounced slowing of his chomping jaws. Paha opened his mouth one last time and fell on his back, teeth gleaming in the sun. He pointed to his open mouth and imitated his hand plucking one of the big triangular teeth from the shark's mouth. Then he jumped up and danced around while whooping it up and shaking the spear over his head.

It was clear Paha had once been part of a lucky group of village men who had killed a great white shark after it swam up the river chasing a seal. Paha made a motion across his stomach and acted like he was eating the shark. His big grin and exaggerated chewing indicated to Frederico that they had eaten the shark and that it tasted delicious. The boy turned up his nose and gave Paha one of those yucky looks that suggested he considered sharks inedible.

Paha laughed at Frederico's sour face. His years as a native had given him a widely varied palate of tastes. Shark meat was just one of many animals he had eaten during his lifetime.

A loud grunt from over the hill caught Paha's attention and he stopped laughing. Peering over the sandy dune he saw the source of the noise. A mother grizzly bear and her two cubs emerged from the brush on the opposite side of the river hungry for a fish dinner.

Paha motioned for Frederico to be quiet as the two of them spied on the big cinnamon colored bear. Her cubs, probably less then six months old, watched as their mother charged into the river and swatted a big salmon clear out of the water. The cubs pounced on the steelhead and ripped it to pieces, relishing every last bit. The mamma bear chased another fish, grabbed it with her mouth and waded to shore. In a few licks she had peeled the skin off the fish and sucked the entrails into her mouth with a big slurp.

Paha nudged Frederico, quietly pointing to the bear cubs and making the same motions across his stomach followed with a very long 'mmmmm' as he licked his lips. There was no question about his meaning. He favored fat bear cubs as a food source and obviously considered them a delicacy.

The wind shifted and almost instantly the big bear caught the scent of the humans less then a hundred yards away. Her eyes peered in their direction but she couldn't make out their obscure forms. Non-deterred she stood on her hind feet snorting the wind and snapping her jaws in a threatening manner. Unnerved, she barked a warning to her cubs and the three of them scrambled up the opposite riverbank out of sight.

Paha was unusually cautious as he quickly gathered the salmon in the carrying net and his fishing spear. They retreated from their riverbank positions and made a beeline for his tule hut. Paha kept turning and watching behind them, hoping the big bear had not followed them. Paha did not want to have a violent confrontation with the family of bears. The good spirits must have been with them because the bear never did appear on their side of the river. Without adequate weapons the two humans wouldn't have stood a chance.

Paha paused for a minute, satisfied the bears had gone in the other direction. At this spot two large sandstone boulders were propped up on top of each other and strange markings and carved cupules completely covered them.

Frederico was curious about what those markings meant. He pointed at them and touched them, feeling their formed ridges.

Paha's face contorted when he saw Frederico's curious look. Those markings were significant to Paha for good reason. At one time they marked the boundaries of his village land.

Dating back to ancient times these pit and groove carvings predated the paintings that also covered the boulders. Many generations ago the first natives to settle this site took possession of the land. Their territory was disputed several times over the centuries by neighboring villages and several mock battles were fought over it. One of these battles resulted in the arrow scars on Paha's shoulder.

Then the soldiers came and claimed all the land for the missions. Now the ranchos claim the land that was once the missions for themselves. The ranchos fail to realize or ignore the fact that the natives were here first and had claimed this land already.

Paha decided to leave what was done alone. The boy's family had taken possession of his tribal lands. It wasn't the boy's fault or even Frederico's father and there was nothing he could do about it. Only Paha remained in the vast region that was once his village territory. What was once his was no more and this hurt Paha deeply but he knew there was no turning back.

The native reflected on this sad fact for a few minutes then left the area with Frederico. Some things were best left unsaid.

They arrived at his tule hut exhausted from their long trek. Paha made a motion with his hands to his mouth to see if the boy was thirsty or hungry.

"Thank you Paha," Frederico responded wearily. He found the stone cup the boy had been using and poured him several cups of water. While Frederico rested, Paha cleaned the two salmon. They were destined for the special pit he used for smoking meats.

Paha retrieved some dry limbs of rotten oak. The pit with the smoldering fire was uncovered and the fish were split, cleaned and placed on a small rack over the fire. He poured water on a rotten branch to produce more smoke and threw it in the fire pit. Clouds of steam and smoke billowed up. After the fire had died down the racks of salmon were placed out of the direct sun. When they were completely dry Paha would eat off them for weeks. Dried smoked salmon was one of his favorites.

The sadness of losing his native lands and the fear of the big bear drifted away with the afternoon breeze. Paha and Frederico shared a special friendship. Their contented look was all the proof you needed to see that.

Frederico left later. As expected, Alou met him near the rancho corrals. She liked Frederico's new attitude and upbeat smile. This was something she could get used to.

Paha was full of hope. Frederico was progressing faster then he had expected and his enthusiasm for native ways was impressive. It gave him a pronounced spring in his step. Something Paha thought he had lost forever.

Frederico liked Paha. He represented all that was missing in his life and he filled Frederico with the spirit of adventure and excitement. Life had not passed him by after all as long as he had Paha.

≋ 15 ≋

      Frederico made himself busy on the rancho the next few days before asking Alou,

      "Alou, please come with me today. I think your father would like to see you. The last time I was with him we stopped by these odd carved rocks. He saw me looking at them and became disturbed. Maybe he's lonely for someone to talk to."

      Alou didn't take long to decide.

      "Yes Frederico, I think I will go. My father gets very depressed about the changes happening around him. Those rocks you saw were the old boundary markers for our village. When the missionaries came they took all our land as their own. When the ranchos came, they also took our land as their own. What he couldn't tell you was that your rancho sits entirely on our ancient village lands. Your family has taken what was once ours. Of course the missions took it first but my father still thinks this land belongs to him," Alou explained.

"Oh, I see why he was sad. The Mexican government granted my father this land but it was never theirs to give," Frederico acknowledged.

"I feel terrible for Paha. I hope he understands," he added.

"He does. None of this is your fault. He knows that. On the contrary, because you are a part of this land, he asks only that you respect where it came from and be grateful for the bountiful blessings bestowed upon you," Alou told him.

"I promise to love and respect this land. Alou, please make sure Paha knows this when we see him today?" Frederico added.

"Don't worry Frederico. My father has seen your spirit and knows you will hold up high that which is sacred to all," Alou revealed.

Alou always insisted on taking a different route in to the village. Today in her haste, she left a trail of broken branches in the direction of the old village.

They tied their horses to a tree and walked 1/4 of a mile to the village. Frederico felt they had come too close with their horses but didn't say anything.

On the way they passed the elevated plateau that made up the cemetery. Alou couldn't have anticipated what havoc her momentarily lapse of judgment would reap.

"Paha!" Frederico called fondly. The native emerged from the back of his hut holding an arm load of animal traps. Piled in the sand behind him were cordage traps of all sizes and shapes. Some were in excellent condition but most needed repairs.

Alou greeted her father warmly with a big hug and a squeeze. They talked quietly between themselves for a short time. Occasionally, they would both look over at Frederico and smile. When they finished their intimate chat Alou called for Frederico to come over by them.

"Frederico, my father wants you to know he casts no blame on you for the things that have happened. You are his friend and that is the way it will always be," she said with a big smile.

Frederico ran forward and embraced Paha, holding him tight. Paha returned the beautiful act of devotion and Alou stepped in for a loving group hug.

Frederico's curiosity finally broke them up.

"Alou, what are all those things your father has piled up behind the hut?"

Alou responded,

"Those are animal traps. Old ones and new ones but not all of them are ready to be used. My father wants us to help fix them."

The boy was honored to help.

"Sure, I'd love to help," Frederico offered happily.

Alou sat down and showed him the thin pieces of native cord that had knotted noose hoops on one end.

"These are bird snares Frederico. See this noose, a trigger stick is tied a few inches from the loop end. You set the snare by putting the trigger on an acorn in the center of the noose. This end loop was secured to the ground by four thin sticks tapped in very lightly. A fifth stick, notched and driven into the ground, held the trigger. The bird would peck the acorn and move the acorn. The other side of the string was tied to a springy stick that had enough whip to catch the bird around the neck in the constricting noose."

"Where do you put them?" Frederico wondered.

"Lot's of places. The more you put out the better your chances. Paha must have fifty of these," Alou said as she pointed to the pile of bird snares.

"Help me check these. Make sure the knots are strong and the noose slips easily," she added.

They quickly went through the pile of traps and checked all the working parts. When they finished Alou moved on to the next pile. These cord traps were bigger. Alou told him they were for bigger game like rabbits and squirrels and they even used them for ducks and geese. The spring sticks were larger and the cord heavier but the design was basically the same.

Some of these traps were in need of obvious repair. Alou asked Paha something and he pointed to his hut. She went inside and a moment later came out with a basket filled with twisted cord coils of all gauges plus what Frederico recognized as asphaltum. She also had a little sack that contained pine pitch.

Paha had traded for the asphaltum cake many years ago. He called it 'woqo'. The pitch had been collected from a stand of Monterey pine trees to the north. Alou took a small amount of asphaltum and boiled it in a clay pot. She added a generous amount of pitch and stirred it briskly. The resulting glue like substance worked very well as an adhesive. Frederico couldn't resist touching the sticky mix.

"No, don't!" Alou tried to warn him but she was too late.

"Ouch!" Frederico cried as he yanked his hand back, a hot drop of the native glue still stuck to his finger.

"Ow, ow, ow!" He continued to yell as he tried to wipe it off his finger. He looked up at Alou with a humiliating look and started to laugh.

"I tried to warn you. We apply it with a glue stick," Alou whispered. She held up a foot long stick about an inch in diameter, dipped it in the melted glue and twirled it around. When a small gob of glue formed she pulled it out and set it on a rock with the hot end dangling slightly over the edge.

Frederico sighed, displeased with his own stupidity. For the next two hours they re-knotted spring snares and glued frayed pieces.

Paha studied his degree of dedication and liked what he saw. In Paha's mind, the young rancho boy was the only suitable candidate for his knowledge. Bright, curious, and respectful, Frederico took things seriously. His reverence for the spiritual side struck the native as highly extraordinary. He had never seen this before in someone so young. This was one of the reasons why Frederico brought such joy to Paha and Alou.

Frederico finished with the traps and stopped to rest for a few minutes. Paha and his daughter were talking nonstop, enjoying the pleasure of hearing their native tongue. The conversation must have been funny because they laughed a great deal. She was probably telling her father about Frederico and his moment with the glue.

Near the end of one of their funny stories Paha motioned to Frederico and asked Alou a question. She thought it was a good idea and shook her head in agreement.

"Frederico, my father has much to teach you in the ways of nature," she laughed, referring of course to the boy's impatience.

"Paha wants to teach you more about the hunting methods of our tribe. He's shown you how to fish and hunt for small game. Now my father, who has many other kinds of hunting implements, wants to show you how to use them.

Paha disappeared inside his hut for a minute before

returning with what looked like a large curved flat stick. In his other hand he had a leather pouch with a long string of sinew attached.

Frederico's eyes opened big and he stepped up to see what Paha carried. Alou sat under the shade of a tree and relaxed, confident her services would not be needed for a while. She wanted to take a nap so Alou phased out the rest of the world and soon was snoring.

Paha didn't need Alou to translate. His throwing stick demonstration would be simple enough for the boy to understand. Especially the basic technique on how to throw it.

The rabbit stick had been cut from a scrub oak during the full moon. Originally close to four feet in length, the slightly curved, knot free branch was dried then whittled flat and shortened to about three feet in length. The blade width was about two inches across and about one inch thick. The inner edge was tapered to a sharp edge and the outside edge left rounded.

Paha held it out at arms length allowing Frederico a chance to look at it. The boy grasped it and waved it back and forth blunt edge first. Paha corrected his hold so that the sharpened, inner blade faced his prey. Frederico made a few hacking motions with the stick not completely understanding how it was used. Paha noticed the boy's confusion and took the stick from him.

He held the stick out to the side and swung it back and forth using his wrist to cock it. With a smooth side arm delivery Paha flung the rabbit stick along the surface of the ground with lots of spin.

The stick whistled parallel to the ground for over seventy-five yards. Paha motioned for Frederico to go get it. The boy took off in a sprint across the flat terrain and returned begging for a chance.

"Paha, can I try it?" He asked. The native needed no translation. Paha stood behind him and helped him assume the correct throwing posture. With his arm to the side and his feet squarely under him he showed Frederico how to sweep it back and forth to get a feel for the size and heft. Paha made sure the boy cocked his wrist and overemphasized the spinning effect.

Paha backed up a few feet and watched Frederico as he took a bead on the sagebrush about thirty yards in front of him. Flinging it with a quick flick the rabbit stick swirled across the ground about two feet high and hit the bush at its base.

"Wow!" Frederico chimed.

"That was easy," he added, full of youthful bravado and confidence.

"Let me try it again."

He ran over to the stick and took aim at another bush slightly farther away. Only this time his feet were splayed out, the stick too far overhead, and he did not spin it. This second throw, without benefit of Paha's positioning, hit the ground in front of him awkwardly.

Frederico flushed with wounded pride. In his haste he had forgotten how important the proper throwing position was.

"Okay, maybe it's not so easy after all," he admitted sheepishly.

Paha giggled, amazed at the boisterous nature of the boy and how much he had changed. A somber, frightened waif devoid of spirit had become this happy excited young man. The transformation filled his heart with respect for the spirit of revival and the undying psyche of the human soul.

This time Frederico took an extra moment, adjusted his feet to bring them under balance, lowered his arm very low and gauged the angle with a few practice swings. Paha signaled him to flick his wrist very hard.

Frederico wound up and gave it a knee low sideways flip, twisting it for maximum spin. The throwing stick sailed in a perfect arc inches above the ground. Spinning at a high rate of speed the stick clipped off the bush at almost ground level. Thrown perfectly, the stick was obviously a potent addition to anyone's arsenal.

Frederico ran and retrieved the stick. It was unblemished by the impact. He also brought the dry sagebrush with him to show Paha the impact point. Happy with his swift mastering of the throwing stick Frederico looked over at the other thing Paha had brought from his hut.

Paha figured the boy was bored with stick-throwing, maybe prematurely, and wanted to learn about his sling. This suited the native just fine because he knew all things took time and practice to perfect. Frederico could master the stick later and perfect his aim enough to learn the subtle art of leading a bounding rabbit.

Alou woke up from her nap. She stirred a few seconds then scrambled to her feet.

"Frederico, I saw you throwing the stick. Your shouts of joy were music to my ears. I'm thrilled for you. When I was a girl, before the mission soldiers came, everybody in our village practiced throwing in the dry riverbed. There were lots of jack rabbits back then and we became very good at hitting them. I'm glad you found it so easy. Has Paha shown you the sling yet? That was my favorite. I was better then some of the boys. Paha made a smaller one for my frame and worked with me on the technique. I was pretty good. Can I show you how to do it? I think I still remember," Alou offered.

She said a few things to her father and he handed the sling to her. For centuries her people used the sling against birds and small game. The stunning blow was deadly at close distances.

Alou examined the sling and told Frederico,

"Look, come closer, I'll show you how this was made. This pocket is made of deerskin but elk skin was the preferred pouch material. My father trimmed the patch narrow at the ends and broad in the center. The whole patch was about four inches long and two inches wide. He poked a hole in each end for the strings. They're made from fiber cord and are close to three feet long. Look, see how he looped the ends of the strings through without tying. This ensured there would be no weak links near the pouch. One of these strings has a finger hold weaved into it, see," Alou described,

"The other has a knot tied a short distance from the end."

Frederico was on the edge of his seat, intrigued by the simple weapon. Alou placed a rounded stone in the pocket and folded it over. With her middle finger inserted in the loop and her thumb and forefinger holding the knot at the end of the other string, she demonstrated the ready position.

Frederico was taking careful note of every detail. He didn't want a repeat of his embarrassing rabbit stick incident.

Clearing some distance between herself and Frederico Alou took aim at a patch of dirt nearly twenty-five yards away. She twirled the sling in a clockwise direction three times around her head. On the third revolution she whipped it around extra hard and let the knotted string go. The two-inch rock sailed far and fast striking to the left of where she aimed. Alou put another larger rock in the pouch and repeated the circular motions around her head. She was quite adept at the twirl. This time, when she released the string, she said,

"Ummph. Yea!"

The three-inch rock flew directly at the dirt spot she was aiming at and kicked up a puff of dirt. She let out a good-natured whoop and handed the sling to Frederico. The boy fastened the string to his middle finger, and grasped the knot on the other one. Alou found a round rock and gave it to the boy. Frederico placed the stone in the center of the pouch and folded it in half. He twirled the sling three times around his head and let it go. He waited slightly too long on his release, sending the rock flying far to the left.

"Oh, ummm, that wasn't too good," he said.

"Here's another rock, keep trying," Alou coaxed.

Again Frederico followed her directions and let it fly. The second time he let it go too soon and the rock strayed to the right considerably.

"One more time," Alou encouraged.

Frederico chose a somewhat bigger stone from Paha's collection and wrapped it snug. He whirled it around and released it with his own heave ho.

"Ahhh, hit it!" He screamed in his high-pitched voice. His big round rock flew high in the air, arced perfectly back to earth and smacked the big stump hard. A big piece of bark flew off from the impact.

"Good shot Frederico. That hit hard. If that stump had been a coyote or maybe even a small deer, you would've busted some bones. What do you think of the sling now?

137

Pretty powerful, right?" Alou laughed, her own adrenaline pumping from the thrill.

"Yes Alou," Frederico responded, obviously very impressed.

∾ 16 ∾

Paha told Alou some encouraging words about Frederico and she immediately passed them on to the boy.

"Frederico, my father is impressed with you. You are a natural he says and he's so sure of your ability he wants to take you on a deer hunt this afternoon. He says it won't take long. He uses a more powerful bow for deer and wants to show you how to use it and also how to use camouflage to get close enough for a good shot. Paha promised to get you back to the rancho before dark. What do you think? Do you want to go?" She said.

"Are you kidding? That's been my dream from the start. Tell him I'd love to go. I'm ready now if he is," Frederico begged hopefully.

"Okay Frederico, let me see what he wants to do," Alou responded.

Paha talked to her quite boisterously. He seemed very excited about the upcoming hunt. In his lively discussion he kept holding his hands over his head. The way he splayed his fingers reminded Frederico of deer antlers. He saw those deer with the antlers regularly in the brush but could never get very close before they sensed him, heard him, or probably smelled him.

Small groups of fifteen to twenty deer fed on the natural grassy meadow in the vicinity of the old village. Later in the afternoon, before dark, they would come out to feed and drink. If the moon was bright they'd feed all night and be bedded down before the sun. Sometimes you could see them in the afternoon sneaking a drink from a spring or the lake. Early in the morning, at first light, was also a good time to see them.

Paha had a favorite place to hunt the young deer that came out late in the afternoon. They were not smart enough to wait for the cover of darkness and sometimes could be fooled with wile stalking techniques and natural camouflage. Paha wanted to show the boy how it was done. Delighted the native man skipped into his tule hut, rustled around inside for ten minutes, and came out dressed in one of his outlandish costumes. The boy stumbled back a few steps startled to see such a change over. Paha had donned an elaborate deerskin cape, complete with antlered deer head.

Alou congratulated her father on his beautiful cape. She had never seen this one before. Her father welcomed the praise, preening himself and striking his great hunter pose. Paha's funny side took control and he started prancing around on all fours like a deer. The natural movements closely resembled the stop and go motion favored by deer and Paha was having a jolly good time doing it.

By the time he finished his deer dance Frederico and Alou were left laughing so hard they nearly cried. Paha enjoyed every minute. He loved being on center stage and the focus of all the attention. Paha pranced over next to Frederico and started nibbling on his toes, drawing one last burst of sustained laughter from all three. Proudly he displayed the cape.

Paha had preserved the head, back, and most of the shoulders of a large deer. A small skullcap supported the antlers while the cape was cut and laced to fit perfectly over the top of Paha's head and back. The skin hung down to the ground on either side of him duplicating the formal image of a deer.

"Alou, the decoy headdress is unbelievable. When he went down on all fours he looked exactly like the deer we see in the bushes. Now I see how Paha intends to get close enough for a shot. Does he have one for me? I would like to wear one too," Frederico asked, hoping his good fortune continued.

Alou asked Paha who nodded affirmatively, but after a short discussion Alou turned and explained.

"Frederico, my father does have another deerskin cape but he wants you to observe the first time. Stay behind to keep from spooking any of the deer. If you see him starting his stalk you are to remain motionless behind a bush or tree and just watch. Pay close attention to the way he stops and goes. He'll be crawling slowly with his left hand on the ground while the right one carries his sinew-backed bow and several chert pointed arrows. Watch as he lowers and raises his head. He'll be pretending to eat grass then raise his head to look around for signs of danger. Deer like to turn their heads from side to side to see if a predator is sneaking up on them. Pay attention to the direction of the wind. You'll want to approach on the downwind side.

Their senses are very good, but sometimes they can be

lulled into a sense of trust if the stalker is good enough," Alou told him.

"Oh, I understand. Make sure you tell him I'd like to stalk with him sometime. I trust he'll know when I'm ready," Frederico accepted wisely.

"How close will he need to get?" Frederico asked, unsure of the range necessary for a good shot.

"My father tells me he has approached to within inches of a rut crazed buck and actually reached up and touched him. It was only after Paha spoke to the animal that the beast realized who he was. Paha said he laughed so hard the deer got away," she related.

"Will he be using the self bow?" Frederico wondered, adding,

"I don't think the self bow is strong enough for deer."

"No," Alou responded,

"My father will be using one of his sinew backed bows. He uses them on large game and, at one time, in mock battles. They're extremely powerful and will dispatch a deer with ease, especially at close range. Did Paha show you his sinew backed bow and arrows when you went rabbit hunting?

"No, he never showed me. I'm really interested in seeing the bow and arrows you're talking about," Frederico related.

The old native made the decision to include Frederico as an observer. Paha ventured within his tule hut and emerged with his deerskin cape under one arm and a sinew backed bow and quiver of composite arrows under the other. His deer bow was slightly less than four feet long and made of toyon wood. Alou had described the bow to Frederico earlier, pointing out the big differences between this bow and the one he had used for rabbits.

"This bow was bent using hot water, not fire," she told the boy. The middle of the bow was curved and the tips were curved."

"Paha bent this one over time and took the greatest care in fashioning this bow. The sinew wrapping was laid in strips over smeared pitch. More sinew was wrapped around the bow to increase the bending strength. This bow worked best with composite arrows," she said.

Paha pulled out a three-foot long arrow from his deerskin quiver. Tipped with chert arrowheads and attached to the foreshaft with sinew and asphaltum, the arrow was an elaborate example of Paha's most deadly weapon. It had sinew wrappings and spiral feather fletchings trimmed with a hot coal.

Frederico noticed that these arrows were different from the wood-tipped rabbit arrows. These arrows were two pieces joined together. The fletched end was of Carrizo cane, dried and perfectly straightened. The arrowhead end was made of a slightly thinner hardwood fore shaft hardened in the fire. One end was inserted into the hollow cane and secured by sinew and asphaltum. In the other end of the Carrizo cane a hardwood nock was attached with sinew and their special glue.

The resulting arrow was a masterpiece of workmanship and skill. Paha had dozens of these arrows. Vigilant maintenance had kept these arrows in perfect condition. Mixed in with the chert arrowheads were a few tipped with flint and black obsidian. One arrow was different from the others. It was painted with red markings and looked more ceremonial then utilitarian.

"Alou, why is this arrow so different from the others? Look at all the markings. Did Paha make this one?"

143

Frederico asked, bombarding her with more questions then she could answer at once.

"Yes, my father made the red arrow. It's a trouble arrow and you're right, it is used for a different purpose. My father made this arrow and left it as a warning to the mission soldiers many years ago. It was supposed to have been viewed as a potent sign of the supernatural powers the mission soldiers faced if they messed with him. The newcomers hadn't the slightest idea what it was and ignored it. As you've heard the soldiers were not intimidated and the revolt ended badly for us. My father still felt this arrow had special power so he retrieved it on his flight to freedom. The spirits told him he would have a use for it many years later so he saved it," she explained, adding,

"My father is an excellent deer hunter and has been since he was a boy. Once his father let him taste the deer ears and he's been hooked on them ever since."

"How do they cook the ears?" Frederico wondered, not even fazed by the mention of such things. He had seen enough of the native ways to know their methods were different then what he was used to.

"Roasted deer ears were a delicacy in my day. After the hunt the men would cook them over the fire, one of many customs we followed when it came to hunting," she said.

"What about the rest of the deer. Did they cook it whole? What did they do with it?" Frederico asked, curious about how they prepared the deer meat.

"Normally they skinned and gutted the deer and placed the heart, liver and stomach in a bag for roasting later. The bones were crushed for the marrow and the sinew used for bowstrings. They would remove the brain for use in tanning the hide and most of the time the tongue and eyes were roasted along with the ears. Any meat that was not going to be eaten immediately was smoke cured and stored in baskets. Because my father was the Shaman our family always received the biggest piece. We shared what was killed with all the villagers. In this way we made sure the entire animal was used. Nothing was ever wasted," Alou explained.

"The deer were gifts from the spirits, Frederico, and we always gave thanks for the bountiful land," Alou added.

Frederico was lost in thought, puzzled by her comments about the brain.

"Did you say they used the brain for tanning the hide? Why was this done?" He asked.

Alou answered,

"Frederico, feel Paha's deer cape. Notice how supple and soft it is. There is only one substance that can make it so soft and that is a brain tanning solution.

Let me tell you how we tanned deer hide. We started the skinning process by making a small cut with an obsidian knife. The rest of the skin would be removed without nicks. Then we soaked the hide in a wood ash solution for four days. This helped remove most of the remaining mucus on the skin. When the hair fell out easily the hide would be taken out of the solution and rinsed off. Any hair or fat that remained was scraped with a deer bone scraper. After scraping, the hide was rinsed thoroughly in clear water overnight, wrung out and left damp for the brain solution. Raw deer brains were put in hot water and worked until all the brain fiber was out. We took the brain water and rubbed it into the hide. It had to be warm to work. When it cooled we would throw it out and start with fresh brain water. We worked the hide with this solution from one side to the other until it was soft. After we treated the hide with the brain solution it was rinsed in clear water, dried out then stretched, rolled and rubbed for hours until supple.

Usually, by this time, the hide was soft and pliable. Other villages and tribes varied the process but ended up with the same thing, a soft deer skin worthy of pride and admiration."

Frederico had been listening patiently. Not every step was memorized but the essential points were not lost. Paha was anxious to get going so they gathered up the deerskin headdress, his sinew backed bow and quiver of arrows and left together.

Paha and Frederico were upbeat about their hunt. The native knew a good place to start on the other side of the lake. He took them to an area that was lush with tender tree shoots and grass. The wind was in their faces as they started their hunt. Paha found a great lookout position and sat down.

Frederico sat quietly by his native friend. One hour, then another rolled by with no signs of a deer. They moved to another vantage point overlooking the small meadow and waited. The entire time neither one of them spoke or moved in a haphazard manner. Frederico was beginning to get frustrated.

Paha never once showed any signs of anxiety. He seemed totally unconcerned with the absence of game. Experience had taught him worrying took away part of his concentration, leaving less then enough to complete a hunt successfully.

They were out in the brush for about three hours when Paha nonchalantly stood up, stretched, and started back to the hut. Not every hunt ended successfully and Paha was patient enough to accept it. Frederico's disappointment was tempered somewhat by Paha's carefree attitude and, by the time they made it back to the hut, he was happy again.

Alou was waiting for them. She had cleaned up his hut, sweeping it with a broom fashioned from a leafy branch.

"Frederico, did you see a deer?" Alou asked.

"No, we waited for hours but didn't see anything. That was all right. It was fun trying. I learned that not everything comes so easily in life," Frederico responded cheerfully.

Alou smiled. She said a few things to Paha who nodded in agreement, seemingly pleased with the lesson the boy had learned.

"My father is happy you didn't get too discouraged. This was a very important lesson. We must not question the spirits when they deny us. That will only make them mad. Accept their will and thank them for the beautiful things they have already bestowed on us. This is the native way. It works," Alou finished smartly.

Alou and Frederico said their good-byes and left Paha in the dunes. The boy enjoyed his adventures with Paha. Every one taught him a different lesson about life and so far he felt he had learned all of them well.

ᨠ 17 ᨠ

The day after the deer hunt Frederico was awakened in his rancho bed by a vicious slap to the face. The force of the blow bloodied his lower lip. Frederico, stunned, was momentarily blinded. Above his jumbled view of the room he saw the smirking faces of Miguel and Carlos.

"Hit him again. I don't think he's awake" Miguel told Carlos.

Whappp! The sting of the second slap jolted Frederico.

"What...what...what did you do to me?" The boy asked angrily, furious at being treated in such an undignified way.

"Shut up you smelly bastard before I beat your face pulpy. Father has gone for the day and your precious digger Alou is not here to protect you. Tell us where you go during the day!" Miguel ordered, hopelessly enraged.

Frederico tried to get out of bed but Carlos held his shoulders down.

"This is the last time I'm going to ask. Where do you go with Alou? She wouldn't tell me either so I took care of her.

She'll be so tired the next time she sees you she won't even recognize you," Miguel roared.

Frederico saw red. His anger blackened his brain, distancing him from the real world. Summoning all his strength he bucked Carlos off and went straight for Miguel's throat. A fraction of an inch before he arrived, he felt something hard slam into the back of his legs. Carlos had recovered in time to trip Frederico and the boy went down in a heap clutching his leg.

Miguel saw his chance. He sat directly on Frederico's chest and beat the boy's face bloody. It was by far the most brutal beating the boy had ever received. Frederico felt nauseated and started to vomit the blood he had swallowed.

The twins left him like that, telling him,

"That was a nasty spill you took from your horse. It's a good thing we came along and helped you. Otherwise, you might have died. Don't forget that. If you tell anyone what really happened, we're going to take care of Alou first and then we're coming for you. I'll torture you to death Frederico, remember that!" Miguel warned psychotically.

Carlos was bothered by Miguel's threatening tone. Today, Miguel had crossed the line. Carlos didn't know Miguel had that much hate in him. He hoped he was bluffing about torturing Frederico. The twins walked out in the yard and checked to see if anyone had heard Frederico's cries.

"Miguel, did you have to hit him so many times? I thought you were going to kill him for a second. What's got into you? Did you see how he looks? Someone's going to find out. Then what? We better hope he sticks to our story otherwise we're dead meat," Carlos complained.

Miguel scowled, muttered something about digger lovers, and clammed up. Carlos was beginning to understand why Miguel was so angry. Frederico had been unusually happy as of late. No amount of teasing could shake that and this made Miguel terribly angry. How could Frederico be so happy when Miguel was so sad? What was he doing to be like that? Those thoughts had become an obsession for Miguel, causing him to lash out in an effort to lay his misery on someone else. Frederico, smaller and weaker then Miguel, was his obvious choice.

Carlos was afraid of Miguel and knew he went way overboard sometimes. Secretly, Carlos admired his little brother Frederico and the strides he'd been making lately. Miguel, however, was the dominant twin and without supervision, had become a hell raiser. Carlos couldn't let on to his change of heart for fear of taking a beating himself.

Inside his room Frederico was shaken but not too seriously injured. The throbbing in his face hurt terribly and his lip was split but Paha's existence remained secure. Frederico's courage, built up by his special friendship with Paha, had held up against all odds. He decided not to tell his father what had happened.

The little boy washed the blood, sweat, and anger from his face and soul. Remarkably, something far greater replaced it. A genuine concern for Alou and her plight and an overwhelming love for his brothers. For Miguel to beat him like this meant that his brother was more depressed and angrier then ever. This lowest of lows he wouldn't wish on anybody, especially Miguel. Frederico made up his mind to help his troubled brother. Show him a path to true inner joy. Frederico ached, not because of injury but because of the tortured spirit that cried out from Miguel's confused soul. This understanding made Frederico feel more in control of his destiny. He was renewed in the process.

After Frederico cleaned himself and changed his clothes he went outside to deal with the rest of the day. He found the twins giving some natives grief by the courtyard. Frederico smiled at both of them as he walked by. This caught Carlos by surprise. He gave Frederico a look of complete humility and lowered his eyes. Miguel scarcely acknowledged his smaller brother, saying only,

"Don't forget what I told you!"

Frederico assured him he wouldn't.

"Don't worry, I won't tell," he said sincerely.

Later in the day Alou returned from the brick-making pit. She was completely covered in mud and drenched in her own sweat.

"Did you tell them?" She asked gently.

"No, did you?" Frederico replied.

"No. I wish I could've been there to protect you. It looks like you took quite a beating," Alou remarked sadly.

"Alou, my heart mourns for Miguel. Something is terribly wrong with his soul. My spirit tells me to be strong and to never give up so that I may help him out of his hell," Frederico announced with conviction.

Alou was not surprised by his reaction. She knew he was filled with the courage and empathy necessary to survive on this rugged rancho. Paha had taught him well.

Miguel seethed for a while but calmed down enough to be civil. Frederico kept his distance as he scrambled to find an answer for Miguel's depravity.

The Captain rode up on his horse and found his youngest son by the corrals. He asked Frederico to ride out to Cave Landing to pick up something he had left there.

"Frederico, I need you to ride to cave landing and bring back a supply manifest I forgot in the warehouse. Can you do it? I need it today," the Captain asked.

"Sure, I can go. Can Alou ride along with me?" Frederico replied.

"No, Alou has been reassigned to the brick pit. Miguel said she needed a change of pace," his father responded.

"That's okay. I can go alone," Frederico shrugged.

He reached the Cave Landing warehouse shortly before noon. He liked being alone and in control of his own destiny. Being bold and adventuresome, that's what built confidence he found. Frederico located the supply manifest right where his father had told him. In no big hurry to get home Frederico wandered along the shoreline.

On the way back he came upon a beached forty-five foot gray whale. The boy was in awe. Huge gaping bites to her belly indicated a killer whale had attacked it. The foamy waves washing up against her were stained red by the flow of her blood as Frederico watched life cease for the whale.

Frederico thought Paha would like to know about the whale so he took an old shortcut to Paha's hut.

"Paha, it's Frederico. Are you there?" He said in Spanish. Paha came out and greeted the boy warmly.

Through a great deal of wild hand gestures Frederico was able to communicate the existence of the dead whale on the beach. Paha and Frederico hurried back to where the incoming tide had partially submerged the whale.

Paha quickly ran to the whale and hacked off the dorsal fin with a small flint knife. The fin was the most delicious piece of the whale. It was cooked and cured like other meats and the blubber was used as an oily flavoring.

The large dorsal fin was too big to carry by one person. Paha was glad he had brought two carrying nets. Made of knotted, fiber cord they were gathered at the ends with loops

and brought together with a large fiber cord. '
draped across the forehead, back, and shoulder.
used these nets for carrying large amounts of goods.

Paha dug out his knife and cut the fin into strips. He
tossed one of the nets to Frederico and motioned for him
to watch how he filled it. When they were full he used a
short stick to keep it tied closed. Using his legs he lifted the
bulging net up on his back, adjusting his legs for the best
balance. Frederico did the same and off they went slowly
back to the hut.

Close to the trail, Paha stopped and threw four huge
clams into the net. They were perfectly symmetrical and had
thick bases. For centuries the natives had roasted these clams
on the fire and thrown the broken shells onto big piles in the
dunes. Frederico's father was expecting him soon with the
manifest so he said good-by to Paha and rode home.

At the rancho the Captain saw Frederico and thanked
him for being so diligent.

"Frederico, you've always been such a good boy. It's
too bad I don't have more time to spend with you. You've
been growing smart too. You put the rest of your brothers to
shame."

Frederico warmed up to his dad's compliments and felt
his love. This was a feeling Frederico had craved for years.

Alou met with Frederico the next day and told him
she would like to do something special for Paha.

"My father is a simple man. There are not too many
things he wants besides the sacred transfer of his native
knowledge. I know what we can do for him in the meantime
to make him feel special. We can build him a sweat house,"
Alou answered, after pondering the idea for a second.

"What's that Alou? Can we do it ourselves?" Frederico

wondered.

"Yes, in the old days every village had one. They were used daily and were usually made of woven boughs completely covered with mud. Most were large dome shaped structures built partially underground. The sweathouse had a hole in the top to enter through and for the smoke to get out. The dry heat made you sweat profusely. We used flat sticks to scrape the sweat off while we sang, talked and communed with each other. People with illnesses received comfort from the heat. Before the men went hunting they would sit in there to mask their human scent and sometimes the women would use them too. After working up a sweat we would leave and plunge ourselves into the lake. Sweathouses played a major role in the rejuvenation and good health of our people. I'm absolutely sure my father would love to have another one. He once told me he felt closer to the spirits when he sat in them. Build one of these for him Frederico and we'll touch a place in his soul that has needed attention for a long time," Alou suggested.

"I'll help you," she added.

They left immediately and found Paha sitting on a bone stool in his hut. Their plan brought a bright smile to the native man's face. They spent most of the day excavating the old sweathouse behind Paha's hut. After clearing away a wood rat nest they were left with a partial frame of willows. Some of the poles had been broken off at the ground and needed to be excavated for replacements.

Paha went inside his hut and returned with a digging stick. Both men and women used the digging stick. It had a slightly rounded blunt point on one end and a flat chisel like point on the other. A polished rock ring was sometimes twisted on to add weight. Paha's digging stick was about five feet long and two inches in diameter and was made of toyon. The weight ring increased the efficiency of the stick, allowing for deeper penetration of the soil.

Paha handed the large stick to Frederico and a big abalone shell to Alou to use as a scoop. It only took two hours to re-dig the holes for the sweathouse poles. Time was running out so Alou and the boy promised to return the next day to finish it.

At the rancho Carlos was trying hard to be friendly to Frederico for a change. As long as Miguel wasn't around Carlos felt safe to reestablish the brotherly love that had died between them after the move from Santa Barbara. Frederico accepted his brother's friendly overtures and even discussed his concern for Miguel,

"Carlos, for the longest time I thought you hated me. What had started out as good natured ribbing turned into humiliating rounds of torture for me. Now I realize it was Miguel who conspired against me. My heart went out to him the other day after the beating he gave me. We need to help him Carlos. Talk to him and find out what's bothering him. Let me know of his needs," Frederico pleaded.

Frederico's unencumbered love took Carlos completely by surprise.

"Miguel has terrible problems," Carlos admitted.

"I am sickened by his rage and unbelievable anger. Miguel will do anything to prevent you from being happy. Frederico, please understand that Miguel controls my actions and my cowardice prevents me from standing up to him. Just remember that I love you and care for you no matter what. I'm glad you've made such wonderful changes in your heart. I've noticed the difference."

Frederico gave Carlos a long hard hug and assured him

he loved him no matter what.

"Carlos, let's go!" The Captain called from the corrals. Miguel and Juan were already saddled up and prepared for another long day on the range. Carlos went over and left with them.

A short while later Frederico met with Alou and they rode out to Paha's to continue their reconstruction project.

During the last twelve hours Paha had gathered all the materials necessary to finish the hut. When Alou and the boy arrived all three of them jumped right into the task at hand. The rest of the willow frame was repaired and the tule thatch siding was applied. Over this they smeared a thick layer of mud. By the end of the day Paha had put the finishing touches on the short doorway, started the fire inside the sweathouse, and laid out his tule mat to lie on. At last they were finished.

"Frederico, my father hasn't the words to express his thanks to you. He will remember this for the rest of his life. Thank you Frederico for helping my father feel so full of life," she confided.

The native smiled graciously and climbed through the door for his first sweat in more then thirty years.

"Let's go," Alou said, moved to tears by her father's happiness.

They left Paha and trod down the trail. Far behind them they could hear the happy songs of native ways joyously bellowed in perfect harmony. All seemed good for now.

As they neared the corrals Frederico realized nobody was watching the chickens. It was supposed to be Miguel's turn but sometimes he forgot and blamed it on Frederico.

"Alou, we better hurry. I have a feeling there's a problem with the chickens," Frederico squeaked.

"Why do you say that?" Alou asked.

"It's a long story but my father wanted us to keep a careful watch over the chickens until the men killed two coyotes that had been hanging around. Today, Miguel was supposed to watch them but I don't see him or the chickens," Frederico explained.

"Why should you worry? It's Miguel's turn today," Alou questioned.

"That doesn't mean anything. In case you don't know, Miguel has a way of blaming me for all his problems," Frederico said.

Far ahead, Frederico could barely make out the form of his father by the chicken coop. The boy's heart sank when he realized he was livid.

"Uh, oh," Frederico groaned,

"There's my father and he doesn't look happy."

"Frederico!" His father yelled,

"Where have you been? You were supposed to be watching the chickens!"

"I, I, I...," the boy stuttered. His father didn't give him a chance to finish.

"The coyotes killed every one of our chickens. This should never have happened. When we left I was under the impression you were going to handle it. This is the last time I ever trust you again. What were you thinking?" The Captain muttered before turning and riding away in a huff.

Hidden out of sight behind a tree, Miguel was snickering like a demon. He knew it was his turn but he had lied to his father and told him it was Frederico's turn. He forced Carlos to back him up and also made a big stink about Frederico and his whereabouts the last two months. No one seemed to know where Frederico was going. Miguel also told his father he needed Frederico to help him sometimes and that the boy was very uncooperative. Beset with a multitude of problems their father had neither the time nor patience to settle this. Instead, he put Miguel and Carlos in charge of their brother Frederico. Somehow his father hadn't noticed the inhumane way they treated him. This was exactly what Miguel had been waiting for.

Miguel met Alou and Frederico at the door. He snarled,

"So you thought you could get away with it, huh. Father has put me in charge of you. I'm going to make sure you never leave this rancho again. I'll put a stop to your wandering off. Starting tomorrow you'll have to pull double duty in the spinning room. Maybe in a month or two we'll see if you have had enough. Now get out of here before I get mad."

Alou escorted Frederico to the spinning room where she urged him to keep strong.

"Look in your heart Frederico. Be strong. Don't let your spirit fail. Paha will be proud of you and so will I," Alou reminded.

She left him alone to consider her words. Alou knew instinctively Frederico would do the right thing. Her only concern was the unpredictable Miguel. Frederico would have to take a stand eventually and she hoped he had gained enough wisdom to handle it wisely.

The spinning room required constant vigilance and was hard work. There was no time for Frederico to rest. By the end of the day he was exhausted.

"Frederico, Alou wants to talk to you," Juan told him on his way to the blacksmith shop.

"Tell her I'll have to catch up with her later. There's no

time right now," Frederico replied wearily as he climbed to his room.

This scenario was repeated over and over for more then a week. Frederico was worked to the maximum while his legitimate complaints fell on deaf ears. Drawing deeply from within he continued to listen to his spirits and kept his cool. The power in his soul fortified him and no amount of mind-numbing, finger-busting labor could dim the enlightenment that coursed through his veins.

Miguel continued to torment Frederico, tempered only by arranged distractions by Carlos. Miguel still believed his twin brother Carlos hated Frederico as much as he did. Carlos was counting on Frederico's newfound spiritual foundation to crack open the terrible shell that tormented Miguel.

Finally, Frederico was able to beg a day off from work. The Captain had stopped in to see how many wool blankets were ready.

"Father, I need a day off. My fingers are so swollen they can't move," Frederico said as he held them up for inspection. I want to go abalone hunting."

"Okay Frederico, go ahead," his father replied, choosing compassion today.

"Is it okay if I take this blanket? My feet are freezing at night," the boy added.

"Sure, I think you've worked hard enough," his father responded.

Off to the side Miguel cursed his father's intervention. The evil twin decided to take care of things once and for all and implement his plan to discover Frederico's secret.

"Father, can I go with Frederico? I've wanted to go abalone hunting for a long time and I don't think Frederico will mind," Miguel insisted.

Frederico shook in his boots. He needed a protective witness if Miguel went. Someone Miguel would agree to.

"Can Carlos come along? All three of us can carry quite a load?" Frederico whined to his father.

The Captain was preoccupied with something else, but responded favorably.

"Okay, but be careful. All three of you stay together. No accidents, please!" The Captain said.

Frederico sighed heavily. With the twins along he knew he could not take the chance to see Paha. However, at this point, Frederico just needed to get out in nature and feel the wind in his face and the warm sun on his back. Paha would have to wait until things were safer.

∼ 18 ∼

Miguel was surprisingly restrained in his taunting on the way to the beach. He seemed preoccupied with watching Frederico's reactions. The angry twin Miguel seemed to be expecting something. The trip to the beach was uneventful until they reached the thinly disguised side trail that led to Paha's hut.

Miguel noticed Frederico staring over in the general direction of an elevated plateau and a large willow thicket. He seemed way too interested in that place. Miguel noticed the side trail but didn't let on that he had. He couldn't put his finger on what was there so he made plans to find out later.

When the boy saw Miguel's inquisitive glances in the direction of Paha's old village Frederico gulped hard and tried not to look nervous. He was pretty certain Miguel had noticed the side trail.

To break the tension and also to distract Miguel's thought process, Frederico spoke out,

"Carlos, did we bring a net or something to carry all

the abalones. I don't think our saddle bags can carry all of them."

Carlos was oblivious to the subtle differences in the trail. His only concern was to stay on Miguel's good side.

"Yea, we brought plenty of hides to wrap them in. How many do you think we're going to get?" Carlos blathered.

"Enough! Let's move on!" Miguel interrupted abruptly,

"We have a long ways to go. Let's pick up the pace."

Frederico was glad to be moving on. He let out a big sigh of relief and rode down the trail. Miguel paused for a few seconds, looked back towards the hidden village and cemetery, and took his bearings for a return trip.

Further ahead the grassy trail turned to sand signaling the proximity of the beach. It was windy. Blowing sand twisted into dust devils and sandblasted the boy's faces. Cold northwesterly winds, prominent this time of the year, roared through the narrow opening in the dunes. The brothers wrapped their overcoats tightly around them.

They emerged from the sand dunes on horseback and gazed at the wind whipped white caps covering the darkened sea. Despite the chill, the bright sun baked their tan faces, making Frederico sweat.

Down the beach about two miles away, their destinations awaited, three large rocky reefs extending more then a thousand yards into the raging sea.

"Let's go," Miguel barked, still obsessing with the side trail and the unnatural looking plateau. Frederico relaxed, casting from his mind the thought of Miguel discovering Paha. The sea air numbed the tip of his nose turning it a bright cherry red. A mix of salty seaweed and silica permeated Frederico's moist nostrils, overwhelming his sinuses.

162

Far down the shore a frothy roar rolled across the face of the waves. White water fronted the rolling breakers slapping at the shoreline. The slope of the sand soaked up the bubbly edge, leaving a shifting, reflective sheen.

The roar continued, breaking the momentary silence. Each frothy white breaker sizzled as millions of tiny bubbles popped open releasing the trapped sea air.

Right behind the tumbling swoosh of foamy seawater another sequence of wind waves lined up, ready to pound the shoreline.

Frederico loved the beach. The sights and sounds took over his disordered life, commanding his full attention. Today the winds were especially brisk, pushed down from the frigid north by an encroaching storm.

Tears formed in Frederico's eyes every time he faced the wind. He was glad he wore extra clothing plus his heavy leather jacket. His jacket had a rabbit pelt hood and by pulling the pelts far around his face Frederico made a windbreak with a pocket of warm air.

Through the opening of his jacket he could see the reef getting closer but could hear nothing above the roar of the waves and the whistling of the wind. Frederico ventured forth, exhilarated to be in the elements.

Far ahead Paha returned from a trip to the river mouth. His sharp eyes saw the approaching horses so he hid behind a stand of willows along the riverbank. To his surprise he recognized Frederico among the group. Much to his dismay and disappointment he saw there were two young men with him. Alou had told him about the cruel twin brothers who tormented Frederico. The native found that situation indefensible. Their outbursts bothered Alou and made her sad.

Paha wanted to meet with Frederico and explain their spiritual bond. Perhaps, if they abandoned the boy he would have time to visit. Paha decided to shadow then all the way to the reefs. At the end of the trail, before the footpath started, they all dismounted. Paha figured they were going to stay together at that point and left them, intending on returning later to see if the twins were still with Frederico. He would dig a few more tubers by the river while he waited.

"Carlos, come here, I want to talk to you," Miguel ordered. Carlos reluctantly went over to him.

"I saw something back there that looked suspicious. Did you see it?" Miguel inquired.

"No. What are you talking about?" Carlos answered.

"I'll tell you later. Stick by me. Our plans might change and don't let on to Frederico, hear me!" Miguel said gruffly.

Carlos kept silent, fearing the unknown. What did Miguel have in mind? He prayed it wasn't another assault on Frederico.

The rancho boy didn't notice their chat. He was too busy climbing the face of the reef. An ancient native trail cut across the rocks, over the top of the reef, and down to an inner gorge sheltered from the buffeting winds. From there the thin trail circumvented the first reef, cut across the second, and snaked down to the deep gorge in the third reef.

Completely covering the footpath was a thick white blanket of bird droppings. Every step a treacherous challenge. More then fifty feet below him low tide conditions left curved crescents of sand tucked into the ends of the rocky gorges.

From where Frederico was standing he could make out the familiar oval shells of abalone stuck to the walls of the gorge. Frederico walked gingerly along the trail. Deeper then the others and far narrower the cove was only accessible during the lowest of tides. This gorge held a virtual bonanza of huge red shells and hundreds of black and green abalone shells.

Miguel and Carlos lagged behind Frederico. The boy had every reason to believe the twins were going to follow him so he turned and said,

"Carlos, Miguel, I'm going into the third gorge. I can see mountains of abalone down there."

Carlos relayed,

"Okay, go ahead. We're going to check the second gorge. Let us know if you need some help."

Sincerely spoken by Carlos, he had no idea what was in store for them. Miguel had determined where Frederico went during the day. His secret place was at the end of the mysterious side trail and he was going to get to the bottom of it today.

"Carlos, let him go. We've more important things to do. Follow me!" Miguel demanded. Carlos knew his brother meant business. He'd only heard that tone once before and that was when he was beating Frederico.

Without complaining he followed Miguel up the trail to where their horses were. Miguel and Carlos rode back to try and find a certain unnatural looking side trail that led up to a prominent plateau of suspicious integrity.

Part way down the trail to the third gorge Frederico noticed for the first time the dark reddish hues of the ocean. The ocean water, normally a turquoise blue, looked bloody. It was a ominous warning and something inside of him hesitated. But the lure of the abalones was too much of a temptation. Frederico made up his mind to get down there no matter how difficult it would be. He slithered down the face of the gorge slowly and at one point, lost his grip and slid down a ten-foot cliff of slimy brown sandstone.

During countless stormy days the wave action at high tide had whittled the reef face. In some places the cliff face exceeded one hundred feet in height. Here and there the clay seams that rippled through the rocks oozed a sulphur yellow slime. Rivulets of the goop drooled down the sheer sandstone face. Frederico regained his tenuous hold on the crumbly rock face and climbed down the remaining thirty feet down to the small plug of sandy beach. Frederico jumped the last six feet and plunked to the sand, landing on his bony butt.

"Ouch!" He said, as he stood and brushed the sand off. When he looked around he saw so many abalone shells surrounding him he felt like he was in a room of solid abalone. The wet rocky walls, visible only during the lowest tides, were so thick with huge red abalone they literally overlapped five deep. An incredible profusion of shellfish in such a small area. Nature's bounty lay at his feet.

"Carlos! Miguel! Come down here! There are hundreds of abalones. Hey Carlos! They're the biggest I've ever seen!" Frederico shouted excitedly.

"Carlos, Carrrrlos!"

That was funny. He had seen them only moments ago. Frederico wrongly assumed they were working the next gorge and they probably couldn't hear him over the wind.

"Wait until they see these," he gasped happily to himself. The boy took out his abalone stick, a flat sharpened stick of toyon, that he used to pry off the heavy abalone shells. Their powerful suction force was too strong to be pried off by your fingers alone.

He kept popping them off one at a time using his body

leverage to lift them. Once they were at least 25% off the rest was easy.

Alou had given him a knotted carrying net before he left. Frederico was glad she did because he was going to need it. In less then a half an hour he had pried more then twenty abalone off the gorge wall.

"That should be enough," he said to himself. The tide had started to rise and small waves were already lapping at his feet.

"Carlos!" Frederico yelled to his absent brother.

"Miguel?" He screamed even louder, thinking perhaps they were playing a trick on him. Hearing no reply he opened his carrying net. There was room for one more big shell so Frederico inspected the mass of attached abalones, searching for a grand specimen. The incoming waves were now covering the sand where he stood. After one long retreat of the ocean's murky red water Frederico saw his prize. Over sixteen inches long and five inches thick this was the grand daddy of all abalones.

Frederico raced to the spot as the waves retreated. It was low against the rocky wall and was now partially submerged. He took his stick and worked it under the huge edge of the shell. His stick could only pry it part ways up with one hand so he placed both hands on the stick and tried with all his strength. Finally, the foot of the abalone released and part of the shell lifted off the rocks. Frederico gave his stick one last lunge but lost his grip in the process. His momentum carried his left hand forward directly under the huge mollusk. At that precise moment a sizeable wave slammed the shell back against the rock where it sucked down hard, clamping Frederico's hand between the shell and the rock.

In a panic Frederico tried pulling his hand out but was

unsuccessful. He tried again, this time trying to get leverage by shifting his feet, but his nearly prone position left him limited room for maneuvering.

"Help! Help!" Frederico screamed, choking back tears of shock. In his desperate mind a strange voice deep within him told him to look for the raven. His fingers reached for the raven on the string as he fought for his life.

"Please, help me! He screamed as he held his raven effigy aloft. He yelled again and again as loud as he could,

"Please help meeeeee!" He finally screamed from adrenaline charged lungs.

Those three small words carried out of the gorge and cut through the whistling wind like a knife. Paha, on his way back to check on Frederico, heard the frantic call for help and scrambled down the face of the reef with the dexterity of a crab. At times he looked like he wasn't touching the rock face at all.

Forty feet below, Frederico took the full force of a wave directly to his face. The entire gorge was filled instantly with water and for a long count of ten Frederico's face was completely under the water.

Inside his soul the boy clung to life desperate to survive. He held his breath bravely for what seemed like an eternity before finally exhaling above the surface as another, larger wave completely enveloped him, casting him into the darkness of murky seawater. With the tide already over his head and his hand unwilling to budge, Frederico thought his life was over. There was no panic or fear, only a warm, rich up swelling of blissful love and contentment. The last two months had been the most wonderful of his young life. He knew he could pass into the spirit world now without reservation, fulfilled emotionally and spiritually.

The cold water glowed phosphorescent green in the darkening shadows. He was confused for a second and thought his life had passed. Frederico looked up through several feet of water to the dark sky above him and saw what looked like Paha's face. This disturbed him because he never had the chance to say good-by to him. What Frederico thought was an illusion came suddenly to life when the native man thrust his strong arms into the water and lifted the abalone stick, Frederico's hand popped free of the abalone's death grip as Paha swooped up the boy and shielded him with his body against another thunderous wave roaring down the gorge.

Paha wasted no time getting out of there. He wrapped the boy's arms around his neck and secured them with a piece of twisted fiber cord. With power impossible for a man his age Paha climbed out of the gorge using his steel grip and churning toes to scale the vertical face of rock. Paha didn't stop until he reached the beginning of the trail to the rocky reefs.

Frederico was semiconscious. Part of his brain told him dreamily he was safe but the rest grasped for the appropriate knowledge to understand what had transpired.

Paha laid Frederico down on his side and worked his arms to dislodge the seawater that partially filled his lungs. With a cough and a gag Frederico regained full consciousness a few seconds later and opened his eyes. He stared into the face of his best friend Paha who smiled, glad his actions had spared the spirit of his young buddy. Paha covered the boy with layered boughs and within a few minutes Frederico had warmed up enough to signal to Paha that one of his ribs was broken. The pounding waves had body slammed him into the rocks several times before Paha rescued him, breaking the boy's rib in the process.

Paha knew the boy needed to get home right away. A nice warm bed and the vigilant care of Alou would help Frederico through this horrific accident. Paha laid the boy over Frederico's leather saddle, tying him down with the rest of his fiber cords. Skittish of horses, Paha warily grabbed the reigns and led the boy home. The native man ran, never stopping and never tiring. Darkness overwhelmed them within sight of the rancho's corrals. To be so close to the house risked his very existence but Paha knew the critical needs of the boy outweighed his own.

Frederico's father and brother Juan were riding up the trail and before Paha could react they came into view. Non-deterred, the native kept running all the way up to them, willing to sacrifice his anonymity for Frederico's well being.

The look of shock on the Captain's face was beyond description. The same could be said for Juan's. Only Paha was able to act and think correctly. He stopped Frederico's horse and untied the boy. With care reserved only for his beloved Frederico Paha took the boy in his arms and handed him to his motionless father.

The Captain could see the boy was injured,

"Frederico, Frederico,.. what happened?"

The prejudices of his emotional mind distorted the face of reality and he instantly blamed the strange native for his son's injuries.

"Digger!" He screamed in frustration,

"What did you do to my son?"

Paha could not understand him but could tell by the tone of his voice he was angry. He felt exposed and in danger so he turned and sprinted back up the trail out of sight.

The Captain and Juan rode quickly back to the rancho and called urgently for Alou.

"Alou, please help my son. Please, he's hurt bad," the Captain cried with real tears of concern streaming from his eyes.

Alou appeared at the door, took the boy from the Captain's arms, and carried the battered kid to his bed. Around the corner Miguel and Carlos hid, more in shock then fear. They had recently returned from Paha's old native cemetery where Miguel had carried out despicable acts of malice. With the forced compliance of Carlos, they had desecrated every visible grave across the whole expansive cemetery, including Paha's wife.

They only left when hysterical ranting by Carlos about angry native spirits touched a nerve of acute paranoia deep within Miguel's tortured mind. Terrified, Miguel decided they should return to the rancho.

≋ 19 ≋

The Captain had forgotten that Frederico was supposed to be under the twin's care. All he could think about, imagined or not, was the despicable acts of malice the strange native man had inflicted on his poor innocent son. The native man must pay for his cruelty he kept rolling around in his head. By now revenge clouded the Captain's mind, extinguishing his better judgment. Frederico's father needed answers right now.

He burst into Frederico's room looking for Alou and said,

"Alou, I must have a word with you. Alou, listen carefully to what I say. I want you to meet with the native man who brought Frederico back and arrange a meeting. You must have known about him. Someone should have known he was out there. Who is he? Tell me! Miguel has already told me of his suspicions. When Frederico disappears, you're always the last one seen with him. Do you know anything about this? Tell me before I hear it from someone else," the

Captain urged, growing more cantankerous by the second.

Alou knew it was useless to resist.

"Yes Captain, I do know this man. He is Paha, my father, and you are living on his ancient tribal grounds. Through his gracious spirit he has allowed you to remain. My father has been a vital part of this land for all of his 66 years. Through a chance meeting with your son Frederico, a strong friendship has blossomed. Frederico's extraordinary curiosity has been piqued by our native ways and my father has graciously volunteered to teach him. Don't you see the changes in him? Haven't you noticed?" Alou said, visually frustrated with the Captain's ignorance.

The Captain stood there trembling with anger. What did she know of his life? She had no idea how hard it was to run the rancho. Everyone needed to understand the situation and support the drastic measures being taken to sustain it.

"Do one thing for me, Alou," the Captain said through clenched teeth.

"Set up a meeting with Paha today. Make it as soon as possible by the corrals. We have much to discuss!" He ended forcibly.

Alou shook with emotion.

"You'll have your meeting Captain. I'll find out when he can meet with you and I'll be there to interpret," she said.

"You can interpret and I want Frederico there too. Make sure the boy understands the importance of this. No stone will be left unturned," the Captain professed with great conviction.

Alou took one of the rancho's fastest horses and raced to Paha's hut. Her father sat deep in meditation, the significance of the last twenty-four hours set rigidly in his mind. Now that he had been discovered by the rancho men he knew his life had changed drastically. He sought answers to hard questions,

"Paha, the boy's father wants to meet with you today! There has been a great misunderstanding. He thinks you caused the boy's injuries. Frederico is so sick he can't relate the whole story without confusion. He keeps telling his father a great spirit pulled him from death's door. The Captain is frightened and wants to know what really happened. Please find it within your powerful soul to enlighten the boy's father," Alou begged.

Paha immediately grabbed some items from his hut and left with Alou. He wanted to get to the bottom of this. Out of concern for the boy, and for the continuation of the transfer of native knowledge, Paha needed more time to teach him. There was much to do and with the winter solstice coming soon, not much time to do it. Frederico's spirit had been chosen to receive this knowledge and nothing would stand in Paha's way.

Alou rode and Paha ran next to her all the way back to the rancho. When they arrived she left him hiding in the brush outside the corral and rode to the house. Alou found the Captain in the courtyard.

"Captain, my father will talk now. His name is Paha and he is a great man. Please give him his due respect. He is honorable and has come in peace. At the meeting he wants to formally extend an overture of peace. I ask that you hear him out before deciding on his fate. Will you promise him that?" Alou asked hopefully.

The Captain agreed reluctantly, then ordered

"Okay, let's meet now. I want all my sons to be there to witness what has to be done."

The Captain left and went inside to prepare for the big face-to-face meeting. Peace was a long shot after what happened to Frederico and Alou was well aware of this. Someone was going to have to pay for their past transgressions. Miguel, in a bid to deflect blame from himself, told his father a big lie about discovering scores of cattle slaughtered by someone he suspected was Paha.

"We kept this to ourselves to spare you the worry," Miguel lied.

The Captain, in his heightened sense of anxiety, believed the whole story without doubt.

"We'll see what he has to say about that!" the Captain promised in anger. Alou had led him to believe the two men could coexist peacefully. If the cattle slaughter story was true there could be no chance for peace. That much was for certain.

"He's going to pay dearly!" The Captain screamed loudly, startling the twins with his pain and anger.

Alou went upstairs and helped Frederico out of his bed. His cracked rib gave him fits of pain but Frederico sucked up his agony and struggled to make the meeting with Paha and his father.

"Slow, Frederico, take it slow. They're not going to start without us," Alou reasoned correctly.

In the corrals the two groups kept a safe distance between them, casting suspicious glances in each other's direction. It had taken a near miracle to get everyone together. One side wanted peace and the other, vindication.

Alou spoke first.

"Captain, my father comes to you in peace. As a man of honor he proposes a truce, a compromise between you and him. He wants nothing more then to live out his life in harmony with nature and to practice his native ways in peace. When the spirits come for my father he wants to be free of your shackles. His heart longs to soar like an eagle and fly with the wind. In return he promises to avoid contact with the rancho men. As a symbol of his good faith my father has prepared a special offering to be shared by all."

Paha pulled a pipe out of a leather pouch and lit the contents with a glowing coal furnished by Alou. The Captain and his sons looked wide-eyed at the old native, unsure of his intentions. The Captain, feeling very uncomfortable, stepped forward and tried questioning Alou,

"Alou, tell me...," the Captain never finished.

"Shhh, take it now," she said.

The woman held her hand to her mouth and motioned for the Captain to accept the peace offering from Paha. The stately rancho man, ruler of his own domain, hesitated, trying to decipher this act of peace.

Smoke curled from the tubular steatite pipe. A hollow tube, once a mallard duck bone, had been fitted to the end of the stone pipe with bitumen. Use over the years had stained the pipe black. Paha took a long draw that turned the embers cherry red then held the pipe out, motioning for the Captain to take a puff.

After a few awkward seconds the Captain took the pipe, puffed twice quickly, and handed it back to Paha. The native took another long draw and set it down. Frederico looked up when Paha cleared his throat, rose gracefully from his seat and held out his hand. Frederico looked at his father, his eyes begging silently for him to accept Paha's hand.

"Please," he whispered to himself,

"Take Paha's hand and shake it. Complete this solemn agreement."

The Captain was fighting inner demons, trying to decide what was right. Without explanation the Captain ignored Paha's outstretched hand. He had partaken of the pipe as a sign of good will to his son but something deep inside was refusing to let him shake the native man's hand.

The Captain turned to his youngest son and said,

"Rise Frederico, I have something to say to you."

Frederico sprung to his feet. His father winced as he looked uncomfortably at his son. Paha lowered his hand unsure of what was happening.

"Frederico, I'm thrilled you have found new meaning to life and a sense of purpose. What concerns me is your fading relationship with your brothers. They love you and want you to be happy but they can't accept the fact that this old native is having such a profound influence in your life. This is why I must restrict your visits with Paha. Your family must come first, not Paha!"

Frederico gasped, his ultimate fear realized. Outraged, he decided his father must know the truth.

"Father, Miguel has teased me for years and bullied Carlos into joining him. They have humiliated me and disregarded my true feelings and, worst of all, you have completely ignored me in my time of need. I was in a state of total despair when we moved out here to this God forsaken place. Paha has helped me to understand myself and with Paha's gentle teachings, I have come to accept my lot in life. Please don't deny me this freedom. It's been my only salvation!"

The Captain was not moved.

"You are my youngest son," he said harshly,

"You must respect my word as law!"

Frederico shook his head in disgust and hobbled over to

the house. He disappeared inside with tears streaming down his face. In the background he could hear Miguel screaming insults at Paha, baying like a vulgar dog.

"Digger, you're nothing but a digger. Get off our land before we drag you off!" Miguel screamed.

"Stop you fools. He wants peace. Show him the respect he deserves!" Alou cried in response.

Miguel looked at Alou and spewed,

"Shut up Alou or we'll take care of you too!"

The shock of the angry warning stopped Alou cold and blind sided the Captain. Miguel's hatred for her people was unjust and almost rabid in its intensity. She had seen this attitude before and knew there was no derailing it. She turned to Frederico's father and said,

"Captain, please reconsider. My father means no harm."

"Enough!" The Captain roared.

"Enough of this nonsense. Paha must go!" He determined angrily, caught up in his wicked prejudices.

The whole troubling episode caught the Captain by surprise. As Frederico's father his main responsibility lay in making sure his youngest son listened to him. He tried to remain impartial but found walking the tightrope daunting. Juan, a silent witness up to this point, decided now was the time to speak up.

"Father, is this what you want, unchecked aggression against a man who has done nothing against you. He is the last one left of his tribe and has come here in peace. Can't you make room in your heart for a compromise?" Juan countered.

The Captain ignored him, choosing instead to remain bloated in oppression.

"Alou, tell your father he must go and never come back because if he does, we will beat him savagely and force him off!" The Captain snarled. Alou looked down at her feet then over at her father. His face was sad. This was not what Alou had expected. Paha looked over at Alou, smiled weakly, then gathered his stuff and left without saying goodbye. He turned off the main trail, preferring instead to take one of the old native footpaths home.

≋ 20 ≋

Paha needed redemption. The meeting at the rancho had not gone as planned. Much turmoil surrounded the whole sorry affair and he needed to renew his spirit of hope. Paha decided to go where he found the source of much of his drive and energy, the final resting place of the spirits of his wife and all the powerful chiefs and shamans before him.

The village cemetery had become a last refuge for Paha and the closest he could get in spirit to his beloved wife. The slightly raised cemetery behind the old village site was obviously accessible but the soldiers had never found it. Paha believed the spirits had turned the place invisible to protect and conserve the sacred nature of the graves.

He made his way along the nearly invisible trail to the village cemetery. Paha had not been there since the anniversary of his wife's death.

As he came close something made him freeze in his tracks. Cutting across the trail leading directly to the cemetery, were the unmistakable tracks of two horses. Their hooves had left clumps of grass and soil tossed everywhere.

Paha's heart did a flip-flop and an awful wretched feeling crawled up his back and seized him by the neck. Groans came out of his constricted throat.

"Ohhhhh!" He shuddered.

No, he thought, not the cemetery. Adrenaline flooded through his nauseated body jolting his shocked consciousness.

Sprinting through the low brush Paha scrambled up the hill to the cemetery. The horrible scene knocked him to his knees. Spread indiscriminately across the sacred site lay the bones of countless native generations.

For a brief moment Paha's mind blacked out and he fell forward into some cactus. The needles pierced the skin of his outstretched arms, poking him in a dozen places, but the pain didn't register. Trickles of blood ran down his arms as he staggered through the cemetery. All that he held sacred had been destroyed.

Grave markers, the stone slabs and wooden poles of past chiefs and shamans were tossed about haphazardly. Every single monument was knocked over and, in most cases, broken by trampling horses. What he saw next pierced his heart like a flint dagger. The grave of his wife had been dug up and completely emptied of all her personal treasures. Whoever did this had gone directly for the grandest grave. Her marker was elaborately constructed of whalebone ribs and was a virtual shrine of power and prestige. The scattered grave poles, decorated with eagle feathers and shell beads, were reminders of the great deeds these men and women had once performed. Their sacred, incredibly intricate head stones had become a magnet for the thoughtless animals that did this.

Native bodies were buried in the flexed position with their knees tied together and wrapped against the chest. The deceased were placed face down and wrapped with tule matting. Important people had many personal objects added to their graves including steatite effigies, beads, stone mortars, pestles, charm stones, flint knives, musical flutes and rattles. All of these had been picked through and tossed aside. Worst of all, the mummified remains of several bodies had been lifted from their four-foot deep graves and stomped by the feet of the perpetrators. The petite bones of his wife had a long leather reata looped around her spine but her skull, arms, and legs had been broken off in the wild stomping episode.

The total disregard for the sacred remains of his wife drove Paha over the edge. Shrieks and bone shuddering groans filled the still air. The proud native man lost all contact with reality and rolled on the ground, tears and spittle streaking his dusty face as his arms and legs flailed in agonizing emotional convulsions. Eventually Paha passed out from sheer misery. When he came to he was alone. The spirits of his loved ones no longer occupied this place. Scattered in the wind by the complete and utter desecration of their graves.

This nightmare would never end and he knew it. Paha took a short time to regain his physical balance. Shaken to the core, the native began making plans to avenge this outrageous intrusion. There was no doubt somebody from the rancho was responsible. The leather rope left behind was proof enough for him. Outraged, Paha declared open war against the rancho men.

As a signal of his battle intentions to his daughter Alou, Paha took his special trouble arrow out of its hiding place and prepared for troubled times ahead. Alou would know what the arrow meant and, with the spirits willing, join him in his final stand against the newcomers.

Frederico and Juan, who were out checking on rancho business, discovered the arrow the next day. Sunlight filtering through the cattails reflected off a flaked black obsidian arrowhead and caught the boy's attention. Triangular in shape the sharp point had a composite shaft attached at its flared base with twisted sinew. The fire-hardened shaft bore the marks of trouble, however. Painted with red slashes, Frederico knew the arrow had been left on the trail as a signal to Alou of Paha's impending confrontation.

Frederico kicked the arrow in anger and gasped,

"Mother!" Furrowing his brow he feared the worst. Would his father cut off all contact with Paha? Would he be forced to cut short his search for native knowledge? The sheer magnitude of the situation brought a surge of blood to his sweaty forehead.

High overhead the cries of a circling hawk echoed across the coastal mesa. Another hawk, markedly smaller, flew playfully close. The big hawk remained undisturbed, as he soared gently in the breeze.

"Frederico! What do you have?" Juan yapped, adding,

"Are you well?" suddenly concerned with the perplexed gaze in Frederico's eyes.

"We have a problem," Frederico declared with sad, hunched shoulders and sore ribs.

"Paha has returned to the rancho and left this arrow as a sign of future trouble. My father is going to be furious when he hears about this," the boy fretted.

"Why do you have such a fondness for the old native?" Juan gently pried.

Frederico fingered the trouble arrow and ignored Juan's question,

"Juan, say nothing about this for now. I need to find out what this bad omen means. Let me take the arrow, find Paha, and get to the bottom of this."

Juan was in a quandary. He knew Frederico's plea had merit but it went directly against his father's orders. His own soul told him Paha deserved to live any way he chose and that no matter what, it would be better to let the old man be.

"All right Frederico. I'll let you go but promise you'll talk Paha out of attacking our rancho. He wouldn't stand a chance against us and I'd hate to see him get hurt," Juan confessed.

Frederico paced nervously for a few seconds then stuffed the arrow in his leather sack.

"No one must know about this," he said to Juan. Frederico's mind reeled with morbid fear of the outcome. He mounted his horse and made his way to Paha's tule hut. Throwing caution to the wind he raced the last few hundred yards without bothering to cover his tracks. Frederico knew Paha's mental state was fragile and the boy wanted to reassure him that everything was going to be all right.

Near the lake the boy saw Paha scouring the ground, searching for something. Frederico rode closer until he could see that the native was collecting seeds from a plant.

Paha's mind was devastated with the terrible and painful memories of the graveyard desecration. A lasting peace with the rancho had been shattered by this thoughtless intrusion. Paha's psychic wounds leaked like a sieve and the native needed inspired wisdom to deal with his pain and anger. Something extraordinary needed to be done so Paha decided to go on a vision quest to find the answers he sought.

As Paha picked the egg shaped seedpod it broke into four segments. Inside, sacred datura seeds lay cuddled together. Dark and wrinkled, the seeds smelled foul. Paha gathered them in the palm of his hand and placed them in a small pouch. He moved to the next cluster, probing each for a few sacred seeds. Each of the plants yielded between six and eight of the magical beans. After picking through nearly a dozen of the low lying plants Paha stopped.

"Paha?" Frederico called to his native friend. Paha stiffened, freezing at the sound of his name. Slowly he turned his head in Frederico's direction until the boy entered his field of view. For a brief second Paha stared at Frederico out of the corner of his eye. Then, without acknowledging the boy's presence, turned his back to him and finished his task at hand.

Frederico was mute with surprise. Why didn't Paha say something?

"Paha, please!" he cried, frightened at Paha's strange behavior. The native seemed to be in some sort of psychological trance. Frederico backed away, convinced Paha didn't want him that close. Unwilling to leave Paha he decided to watch from a distance.

Paha picked through the seeds in the pouch, tossing aside the majority of them. He ended up with about a dozen viable ones and rolled them in a leaf. Paha intended on using these magical seeds as the main ingredient in a special vision-producing potion.

Early in Paha's training as a shaman he had been taught the identifying characteristics of nearly a score of vision quest plants. His teacher had encouraged him to partake of the mind-altering herbs in order to know the effects of each and to gauge which ones were appropriate for the ritual being performed.

For the powerful knowledge Paha needed he would use the potent datura potion. When mixed with the right ingredients the powerful visions were strong enough to fortify him for the confrontations ahead.

Mixed haphazardly, the potent brew would overtake breathing and cause death by suffocation. Paha's training was his only protection from certain death.

On the way back to his hut Paha stopped several more times to gather more plant materials including small green leaves, a strip of inner bark, and a purple fungus. He added these ingredients to the seeds in his pouch and when he was finished, tucked the mixed bag of plant materials into his hand and ran back to his hut.

Frederico followed and watched as Paha quickly started a fire and placed some small rocks in the flames. Satisfied with the intensity of his fire Paha shifted into high gear. He took all the ingredients from his vision pouch and dumped them in a small mortar. With a long pestle he started grinding hard, stopping every so often to add a fine white dust. After a few minutes of pulverizing, the brown doughy mix was collected in a gob and dropped into a partially filled water basket. He added several small hot rocks from the fire to the basket. They sizzled when they hit the water instantly steaming the basket. Paha dropped one last hot rock into the steaming brew and left the potion to simmer.

Throughout this whole strange episode Paha never once looked at Frederico, spoke to him, or hinted that he knew he was being observed.

This strange mystery baffled Frederico, sending him into a whirlpool of doubt. He had thought his friendship with Paha bridged the wide divide of their cultures. Of course

Frederico had no idea that his brothers, in their thoughtless ignorance, had caused Paha supreme misery by spreading the bones and stealing the personal effects of Paha's dead relatives.

Paha emerged once again from his hut to test the temperature of the water. He dropped one more hot rock into the basket and stepped within the confines of his hut to prepare.

≈ 21 ≈

Frederico kept watching from the bushes for signs of Paha. Strange noises emanated from inside the tule hut and Frederico thought he could hear the low, nasal toned flute Paha played when they went fishing. He had heard the rattle too. Throughout it all the quiet sobbing of a man in turmoil reverberated from within the hut.

Frederico has no idea why Paha was acting so strange. Without Alou to interpret he could only guess what must've happened. The desecration of his wife's grave never entered his mind.

Paha screamed angry yells of frustration, misery at its worst manifested in vocal sorrow. Frederico was shaking and crying now too. His young mind confused by the mysterious lamentations of Paha. Inside his soul the boy's all knowing spirit also mourned.

Frederico heard a muffled, snorted grunt. It was very close to the grunt of a bear and the strange noise kept getting louder and faster in tempo. Frederico wanted to race to the door and release the trapped spirit inside. Suddenly, after a loud incomprehensible scream, the sounds from within stopped. The tule mat doors ruffled open and there stood Paha, clad from head to toe in an elaborately, decorated bearskin.

When the native moved forward Paha walked not as a man but as a bear. He scurried over to an area in front of his hut and began the most amazing dance. Somewhere from within the bearskin covered man strange plunking noises echoed forth in a hollow tone. Every time Paha shook his legs the sound effects startled Frederico, rattling his psyche. The movements so unnerved the boy that he cried out,

"Paha, Paha, What's happening?"

His words came as whispers, not as yells. Paha couldn't hear him. No distraction was great enough to shake him from his trance. Paha kept dancing, grunting like a bear the whole time. He kept flapping his lips and jaws together and made smacking noises with his mouth. Snapping his jaws and pawing the dirt, grunting and snorting, he acted exactly like a bear in turmoil.

Frederico was speechless. He had come to the conclusion that something terrible had happened. A stirring need to watch this, to witness Paha's reactions took control of Frederico's attention. His curiosity stoked by the mysterious dance of the native.

Paha ended with a whirlwind of spinning rolls. Propped up on one knee Paha twirled completely around twice in one direction then three more times in the other. When he came to a stop he lay on the ground and shuddered.

Frederico's heart nearly jumped out of his mouth when he saw Paha suddenly go limp. He feared the very worst. Thirty seconds later Paha stood and assumed his man persona. Very low, in an almost guttural tone, he began to sing a long low song. The sound affected Frederico in a strange way. Deep inside the pit of his stomach a power created a rippling effect that rolled through his body.

Cold sweat beaded on the boy's forehead and his face flushed as a strange light power streamed out of his head, made two loops around Paha's chest, and plunged straight into Paha's forehead. The scene etched itself into the deepest recesses of his mind. Could he be dreaming Frederico wondered?

Frederico hovered at the edge of the brush, ready to fly into Paha's arms at the slightest invitation. The native kept ignoring Frederico even though Paha saw him, smelled him, and felt his powerful spirit supporting him throughout the entire ritual. Paha didn't feel he could include the boy in this most powerful of dances at this time.

They were undertaken to give the dancer sacred knowledge and power. The bear dance was a favorite of Paha's. Once before he had performed this ultimate dance during the revolt at the missions. Now he needed to gather strength for the final battle between himself and the desecraters of his tribal lands.

Paha stopped singing and walked over to the basket containing his brewing potion. The contents simmered, blackened by heat activated chemical reactions. Paha took the basket and poured the warm contents into his carved wooden bowl. He held it up, uttered some incomprehensible chant, and in one long slurp drank the potion. Black stains streaked the corners of his mouth as Paha wiped the spittle from his chin and went inside his hut. When he came back outside he was minus the bear suit but carried a small deerskin pouch in one hand.

Frederico stood erect, placing himself in full view of the old native. Their eyes met and locked for ten seconds. No words were spoken but Frederico could sense the hurt and anger within Paha's soul. The boy seemed to understand his place as silent witness to a process so powerful no words could do it justice.

Paha broke their gaze and sprinted off into the brush with Frederico trailing behind. Near the base of a rocky cliff a clear running creek cut a v-shaped canyon through the hills. Paha had to make it to his sacred vision quest cave before the effects of the potion overwhelmed him. He ran the entire way. Frederico followed on horseback the best he could.

Paha's special pouch held all the paints and brushes he used for painting. Rock paintings in caves represented the shaman's interpretation of powerful images induced by hallucinogenic herbs. These herbs gave the native knowledge and power during times of incredible stress.

Most of the paintings were clustered in caves close to permanent water and hidden behind dense foliage. Their locations were known to only a handful of the villagers. Paha, as shaman, used several caves for rock art and vision quests. Some were more powerful then others and a few had very specific purposes. The most ancient of caves had pit and groove petroglyphs covered with many layers of recent painted art. Colors chosen included their favorites red, black, white, yellow, blue and green. Each color had a special significance. The images included pinwheels, stick figures, swirls, fingers, and geometric shapes. Almost anything, depending on the artist's visions and ability.

Paha was sweating profusely by the time he made it to the base of the pitted cliff. A thick stand of manzanita stood between him and one special cave hidden behind a large bush.

A few yards behind Paha Frederico dismounted and tied his horse to a tree limb. He kept his distance from Paha, not quite sure what was to follow. Slight tremors were beginning to affect Paha's extremities. They started in his hands and feet and radiated towards his torso. His face turned a mottled purple and red and he shuddered violently. Paha knew there was not much time left before the visions completely overwhelmed him.

Frederico was astounded. The potion Paha drank had turned him into a sweaty contorted mass of trembling flesh. The intensity of the effects grew by leaps and bounds as the minutes passed.

Paha approached the edge of the thick manzanita searching for a small spot to crawl under. Frederico was too intimidated to get closer. Finally, Paha found a crawl space and slipped under the brush at ground level.

He slithered under the red manzanita as numerous branches scratched his skin. Impervious to the pain, Paha's dark, dilated eyes kept searching for the cave's hidden opening. He was sweating profusely and the effects of the vision potion were beginning to disorient him. Blinding flashes of pure colors made him gasp in bewilderment. In between the strange nauseating flashes the real world came into view. During these brief periods of consciousness Paha continued to crawl through the thick brush. A few feet farther and the mouth of the cave revealed itself. An old layer of broken branches still laid partially across the opening, put there by Paha the last time he had used this cave.

All at once the real world began to melt around the old native. Flailing his arms against the flimsy branch pile covering the entrance Paha clawed a way in. About ten feet inside he stopped and propped himself up against a wall of incredible rock paintings. After the next wave of nausea passed he fumbled around in his deerskin pouch and found his special paints and brushes.

From a short distance away, directly across from the cave entrance, Frederico peered into the dimly lit cave. He had never witnessed such a spectacle.

In his leather bag Paha found the different bars of dried pigments he would need for his vision paintings. Early afternoon light flooded the cave illuminating the interior rock wall as he laid out his paint cakes, a very small mortar and pestle, some milkweed sap for binding, and small duck feathers to be used as brushes. Paha then closed his eyes and prepared himself for the flood of visions that would dominate his mind. Within seconds they began.

Strange sparkling globes filled the black hemispheres of his mind. Paha saw hordes of small stick figures scurrying around. They looked like flesh-covered ants with bulging bellies. These strange creatures formed a long straight column and were coming straight towards him.

Paha tried hard to interpret the importance of this vision. They must be the men from the rancho judging from the vast numbers of them and they must be grouping for an attack. When he opened his eyes Paha painted a depiction of the strange stick figure ants he had seen in his vision on the rock wall. Painting swiftly the form took shape as he finished one painting then closed his eyes again as a new, more powerful wave of sparkles and flashes flooded over him. His freshly painted stick figures glistened on the wall, the newest addition to the gallery of paintings proudly displayed in the cave.

Outside, Frederico crept closer for a better view as Paha continued to sweat profusely. Puddles of perspiration pooled in his clenched eyes and localized tremors affected his extremities. Paha was experiencing an overwhelming vision. The long column of soldier ants were gone and in their place a huge beast roared in a low monotone and stared with two eyes that shone like a bright moon. Far in the distance a second angry beast moved straight for the first. They passed within inches of each other, separated only by a dotted white line.

Paha had no clue to the meaning of this vision. The bizarre nature of the dream was more then he could understand. He opened his eyes and forced them to adjust to the growing darkness. Paha painted his rendition of the strange moaning beasts on the wall next to the stick figure ants. He carefully traced the white lines on the wall, coloring the box shaped beast in red, with his piercing eyes a bulbous yellow.

Exhausted from the effects of the magic potion, sleep captured Paha's consciousness. His first vision had been revealing enough. Now he needed to prepare himself for the attack by the men of the rancho. Mouth agape, Paha settled fitfully into a fetal ball under the darkening sky and passed out.

Frederico crawled unseen back to his horse and rode home. Many questions remained and his frustration with the situation caused him to sob uncontrollably. He knew something bad was going to happen. His spirit had told him as much. Perhaps his father would change his mind and let Paha stay. He made it home charged with desperation and plodded straight for his room.

He loved his native friend Paha and couldn't stand

the thought of him being driven away. With this in mind Frederico decided to lay down his life, if necessary, to prevent the inevitable.

ᨠ 22 ᨠ

Paha groaned when he woke up from his incredible vision quest. Curled tight as a ball, the native slowly stretched his legs and back as creaks and snaps accentuated his every movement.

The world around him continued to spin in triplet. Paha closed his eyes and squeezed them shut for a second. Kaleidoscopes of color fluttered mutely behind his lids. He pulled together all of his resources and concentrated. Soon the swimming motion in his ears stopped and he dared to view reality.

The world was singular now, a bit dreary and sort of drab. Paha sat up and cleared the cobwebs from his head. Immediately his grave situation became apparent to him. Painted on the walls of the cave new vision images glistened with fresh paint. In a flash the meaning came back to him. The men from the rancho were coming to get him.

Paha pulled his weary body up and, clutching the walls as a brace, sidestepped out of the cave into the brilliant morning sun. He put his arm in front of his face to block the direct rays and slowly acclimated to the bright light before he moved another step. The urgency of his mission gripped him by his throbbing temples. There was no time to waste.

Paha slid under the manzanita and emerged on the other side covered in dust. Somehow he had managed to avoid all the branches that had torn his skin the first time. Running as free as the wind the native ignored his queasy feeling and in short order was back at his hut.

Paha went inside and gathered his warrior weapons. A tule mat in the corner covered them. Unused since 1824, dust caked the top of the mat. First and foremost was his sinew backed battle bow and composite chert tipped arrows. Next, he needed his wooden war club. Paha had carved it years ago from a single chunk of mesquite wood found during a hunt. The perfect burl and branch sported a club head six inches in diameter. He had fashioned a handle twelve inches long, cut an eyehole and laced a fiber cord through it. The club was a proven head basher. Once, after the revolt, a crazed soldier ambushed him near his hut. Paha was able to use the club to protect himself in the violent fight. The soldier suffered a fractured skull and died a short time later.

Paha stood and practiced his thrust. The club was made for thrusting up into an enemy's face. Grasped near the head it was brought up to injure and it could also be used in a downward manner against the skull when you had your adversary by the hair. Paha hung this club from his waistband. After all his arrows were gone he would use it in hand-to-hand combat.

Paha took some of his personal effigies out of his basket, including the killer whale figurine and some rough quartz crystals. He believed these objects would give him supernatural strength.

An outer jacket of deer leather, double reinforced in the torso, would serve as his armor. The last items he gathered were the long flint dagger he carried in his hair, his rabbit stick, and the all-purpose sling. The dagger was a last ditch weapon for close encounters and the throwing stick could double as a club but was better suited for long distance crippling. The sling he brought along in case all else failed.

The time had come for Paha to make his last stand. Before he left he glanced at the hut and the old village he loved so much. Briefly, he thought he might never get to see these parts again. The sad revelation disturbed him but didn't dent his courage.

Approaching Paha's village less then two miles away an angry, incited mob of rancho men rode down the trail. Accompanying them were the twins Miguel and Carlos. Noticeably absent were the Captain and Juan. Frederico raced to catch up. They had tried lying to Frederico about where they were going but the boy sensed trouble and followed them. Frederico wanted to be there when all hell broke loose. Perhaps he could protect his native friend.

After being directed to his hut by Miguel, one of the men on horseback rode ahead to scout the village site. By chance he saw the lone native running up the trail and went back to alert the others. Paha had not noticed the rancho scout.

The malevolent group waited in ambush behind a thick stand of scrub oak as Frederico sprinted. Somebody had to stop them. The Captain was unaware of the lynch mob gathered by Miguel and Frederico knew his father would not have condoned their violent ways.

Paha continued up the trail unaware of the danger

lurking ahead. Close to the time the old native rounded a bend in the trail Paha noticed something very unusual. Ahead, a number of fresh horse tracks veered off the trail. Slowing to a creep he realized there was also an absence of noise. Everything was quiet, way too quiet. Paha's heightened level of agitation intensified his feeling of dread.

Paha stopped dead in his tracks when Frederico came sprinting around the corner on his horse. The momentary distraction prevented him from hearing or seeing the six horsemen who burst from the brush behind him. One of the rancho men threw his rope around the proud native's body and yanked him off balance. The next man knocked Paha down with the shoulder of his horse and then the rest of them got off of their horses and pounded him with their fists and boots. Poor Paha never had a chance.

Off to the side an enraged Miguel screamed,

"Beat him, knock the stuffing out of his digger body!"

His exhortations grew louder and angrier, culminating in screams to,

"Kill him! Kill him! Kill his dirty, putrid soul!"

Carlos and Frederico were horrified at the chaotic scene.

"Stop!" Frederico screamed,

"You're killing my friend. Please, I beg of you, stop this insanity!"

The boy tried to enter the fray but was held back by Miguel. A well placed boot to the face took the fight out of Paha. Knocked unconscious the native fell defenseless. The rancho men kept hitting him and stopped only when Carlos flung himself over Paha's battered beaten body.

Frederico shook free of Miguel's grip and raced over to Paha. He clutched his native friend's shoulders and begged,

"Wake up Paha, Get up. Please God, save his soul. Don't let him die. He's my friend!" Frederico sobbed.

Carlos climbed off of the native and backed away, repulsed at the violent aftermath of the ambush.

"No more, no way!" He choked to Miguel.

"I'm never going to do this again. You've become an animal, a sick, depraved beast of a man. There's something terribly wrong with your soul Miguel and I hope God has mercy on you!" Carlos shrieked.

The rancho men left Carlos and Frederico, caring nothing about Paha's condition.

"I'm sorry, I'm so sorry Frederico. I had no idea it would come to this!" Carlos said remorsefully.

Frederico couldn't deal with Carlos or his apology at the moment. His immediate concerns were for the survival of Paha. The native stirred, too beat up to moan. Under his swollen limbs Paha could see the jut of broken bones. With Frederico's help he crawled to the side of the trail to await death. The trail of blood jarred Carlos, stunning the petrified twin of pure evil.

"Go get Alou!" Frederico begged.

"He'll die without her help! Right this vicious wrong Carlos. Help us!"

The look of shock and dismay on the face of Carlos irritated Frederico. Fear gripped Carlos and he sprinted away in the opposite direction of the rancho, far too disturbed to help anyone.

Frederico's will was tested as he assisted Paha. He knew the native man needed to be home in a familiar place. Using his horse and some rope the boy helped the injured man to his hut. Only after he was safely inside did Frederico leave and race for Alou.

Alou hadn't heard of the assault. When Frederico told her she turned pale and her legs became wobbly. Alou grabbed her bag and returned with Frederico to the hut too petrified with shock to talk.

"Paha, Paha, my dear sweet father. What have they done to you?" She cried in her native tongue when she saw his battered body. Alou fashioned splints from willow sticks and tule matting and went right to work dressing his wounds. She poured her heart and soul into giving Paha relief from the bone grinding pain.

Frederico was shooed away by Alou who realized her father needed 100% of her attention.

"Go now Frederico. Leave us. With the great spirits help he'll survive. Trust me Frederico, my father's ways are very powerful. He'll find a way to survive with help from above," Alou cried passionately, sticking to her determined guns.

Frederico left and returned slowly to the rancho, full of concern for his fallen friend. He saw the perpetrators of this heinous crime milling around the courtyard bragging to one another about how brave they were. They viewed the beating merely as another side note to an already busy day.

Frederico knew there was no dealing with their ingrained prejudices and misplaced loyalties. They'd gone too far and nothing could make them see the evil of their ways.

Frederico went inside the house and lay down on his bed. Mute with disgust he fell asleep with all his dirty, bloody clothes on. He hoped to dream of times past when life was full of the blessings of the spirit but the nightmare of the day remained.

﷽ 23 ﷽

Frederico stayed inside the house for a week, stripped of all joy and the friend that made him whole. He was so disgusted with life he chose to sleep all day and all night, waking only for a rare meal once a day.

The boy felt utterly alone. Alou had not returned and there was no word on Paha's condition. Frederico's deep depression sapped his strength leaving him weakened in spirit and body. His soul was not dead, however. It would never die or give up. Mountains of men couldn't restrain his inner power so Frederico clung to this pillar of hope.

Miguel and the men had lied to the Captain by saying Paha ambushed them.

"In defense of our lives the only recourse was to pummel him," Miguel boasted.

"When that deranged digger came at me with his devil eyes blazing red, I stood up to him and repelled him with my brave heart. It was only after he attacked my baby brother that I had to take matters into my own hands. Up to that point we were going to let that animal live his life somewhere else. If only he'd respected our land. They'll never learn these diggers, they'll never learn," Miguel said contritely.

Back at the tule hut Alou had been there seven straight days and given Paha around the clock care the whole time. More then once she thought she had lost him. She was extremely worried about her father. The medicinal herbs and prayers to the spirits couldn't undo all the damage. Alou was at the end of her ropes. Exhausted mentally and physically, she was unable to sleep, afraid her father would pass away alone. The native woman, daughter, and real friend cried for her father all day and night.

Miraculously, Paha regained consciousness on the seventh day after all the grotesque swelling in his face and head had subsided. Alou had used her father's special curing stone of serpentine on his forehead, keeping it stuck with a small piece of asphaltum. However, the broken bones in his leg and arm were not setting right. She could hear the jagged ends grinding when he shuddered. White hot flashes of pain shook the man to the core and Alou knew he couldn't possibly take much more of this.

Paha's first words awake were,

"The winter solstice is coming. We must prepare."

It was a determined call for something far more significant then his own mortality.

"No, rest now Paha. We'll be ready. Don't worry, I'll help you," she promised.

His feeble words meant more to her then anything. She had no doubts that an unseen force was in complete control now and that the final outcome was safely in the hands of the Great Spirit. A calm, satisfied feeling flooded over her. No matter what happened this was something she would accept and move forward with.

The darkness of death came for him again but Paha was not ready. This time something remarkable happened. When he regained consciousness, Paha sat up and tried to stand, his badly shattered arm tied to his torso with a fiber cord. The black, blue, and yellow tissue all but lost for good. His broken leg had fared much better. Cracked and broken, but not misaligned, Alou's crude splint was helping.

Unwilling to rest any longer Paha put weight on his leg for the first time and collapsed into the supportive arms of his daughter. Alou helped him to bed and tried to calm him down.

Paha kept repeating in a whisper,

"The winter solstice. Who will pull the sun back if I'm not there? Please help me Great Spirit in the sky. Give me wisdom and strength. I must not let my people down!"

Alou was absolutely in a panic. She knew his special winter solstice ritual meant more to her father then life itself. She couldn't bear the thought of his inability to perform the sacred rite. Somebody must help him. Someone close to him and trusted. On this most sacred of days only someone of pure spirit would do.

"Frederico," she gasped to herself,

"He's the only one. Father, listen to me. The great spirits are talking to me and saying Frederico must help you. This boy's soul is the one who can make this happen. Paha, open your heart and mind and let Frederico go with you and give you assistance during this critical time. Once you told me the boy had a special spirit in his soul and that your spirit had given you permission to impart on the boy all the ways of our people. He is your only chance. Listen to me Father, I speak the truth."

Paha opened his dark eyes wide as they blazed with supernatural fire and said,

"Alou, bring the boy. He needs to know about the winter solstice. I trust him. He's my friend, my spiritual son. I miss him. Please bring him to me. His great spirit is needed more then ever."

Alou left Paha and returned to the rancho to search for the boy and his father. Alou found Frederico in bed sobbing softly.

"Frederico, you must come. My father needs you to assist him in the most important ritual of the year, the winter solstice."

"What? Paha's alive? Take me to him. Please, let's go now!" Frederico urged, incredibly relieved to know his native friend was still among the living.

"Frederico, you need to be there for him, but only if you're there freely, without constraint. I must ask your father for his permission. Without it there is nothing I can do. If you go there against the wishes of your father it would be too upsetting to your soul. We have no choice but to seek his permission," Alou explained, adding,

"The spirits told me it had to be like this."

"No, he'll never allow it!" Frederico said in a panic.

"He'll keep me here. I know it!"

Alou tried to reassure him.

"Frederico, the spirits can change the hearts of men at the most opportune of times. My gut instinct tells me this is one of those times. Have faith my boy, we will not be repulsed."

Alou said this with such believable conviction that Frederico became convinced it would happen. He lost all fear as his courage peaked.

Outside the Captain pulled up on his horse, alone for a brief moment. Alou and Frederico rushed outside and confronted him before he could dismount.

"Father, Paha needs me today. I must go. Please say it's okay!" Frederico begged.

"Now just a min...," the Captain was cut off by Alou who presented her own impassioned plea for mercy.

"Captain, you must let us go. My father is dying. He can't hurt you any more. You don't have to fear him. He's a good man and the last member of our village. When he goes our ways will die. Frederico has been chosen to be the caretaker of our sacred knowledge. Captain, listen to me. Search your soul and find that which is pure and good. Use the wisdom and intelligence God gave you to see how important this is for Frederico, my father, and all my native people. The winter solstice approaches tomorrow and my father must perform a secret ritual to insure the return of the sun to its full glory. Without his help our futures are bleak, all of ours. Give us your permission, your solemn word. I ask this not just for my father and our people but also for Frederico. Paha is his friend and when he passes your son's heart will be broken. That time is coming soon."

The Captain was speechless. He looked deep into the pleading eyes of his son and saw something truly beautiful, a compassionate spirit full of joy and knowledge. Paha had helped his son. He understood that now. The Captain told her,

"Go Alou, take Frederico with you. Help your father any way you can. Go now. Ride like the wind and let your loving spirits heap power on Paha. Every man deserves this, even Paha. I hope we are not too late."

Alou had expected this reply. The good in his father's

heart comforted Frederico. He saw something in his father that made him love him with an infinite power. Alou was right. The spirits could change a man's soul. Frederico was overwhelmed by the loving change in his dad and his spirit was filled with joy.

The Captain handed Alou his fastest horse and Frederico jumped atop his own. Frederico felt compelled to address his dad,

"Thank you Father. You've done the right thing," he said loudly as he left in a hurry with Alou.

Alou and Frederico arrived at the old native village late in the morning and rushed into Paha's hut. They found the old native dressed in his best shaman clothes. Special eagle feathers adorned his feathered topknot headdress and crystals of quartz dangled from his neck. Propped up next to him was a specially adorned wooden sun staff topped by a pierced steatite disk. Incised markings separated it into segments, the meaning of which was known only to Paha.

The majesty of this great and powerful shaman shone brightly in the hut, empowering Alou and Frederico.

Alou said something to her father, encouraging him to act.

"Paha, I'm here to help too," Frederico said to the visibly moved native man.

Paha whispered softly to Alou and she quickly looked in a small basket at his feet and pulled out his body paints.

Paha's broken arm prevented him from applying his body paint and he needed their help. Without full body paint the ceremony could not go on. It would not be acceptable to the spirits.

She mixed Paha's red and black paints together with a small amount of water. The resulting paint, striped across his face and upper torso, took on a rust color. Contrasting bands of pure white were painted adjacent to the rust streak. They gave Paha the spiritual look of lore.

Alou worked quickly, using soft feather brushes to apply the body paint. She hurried because they were far from the winter solstice cave and getting there in time would be a stretch with Paha's injuries.

"With help from the spirits even the impossible could be achieved," Alou reminded Frederico.

Paha's ceremonial items were rolled in a small tule mat and tied with a piece of cord. Alou found his old gnarled cane and with a slow lifting motion propped her father up. The boy jumped up to help support him.

Paha steadied himself and sang that long, low song. The song stirred Frederico's soul and released the power of the spirit within him.

Frederico felt a whirlwind of energy rise from his center of gravity and flow straight out the top of his head. Paha kept singing, raising his voice as he gained strength. He sang louder and louder. Then, in a crescendo of strength, he yelled,

"Whoooeee!"

Paha staggered forward, Frederico on one side and Alou on the other. The journey ahead would be a long and treacherous one and Alou knew they couldn't rest along the way. The three of them plodded through the soft sand. At times they carried Paha as he bravely put his best foot forward and ignored the jolting pain emanating from his shattered body.

ᄿ24ᄿ

Far to the south two prominent rocky points extended into the ocean. Tall cliffs dominated the coastline beyond that. Somewhere along this section the winter solstice cave lay. To get to the cave they needed to wade through the river mouth. The exact location of the cave remained known only to Paha and Alou trusted he would lead them to it.

"Come on Frederico, my father's destiny awaits," Alou reminded the dog-tired boy. She herself was laboring and sweating profusely. The searing pain in Paha's limbs kept him on the edge of reality, in and out of a catatonic stupor.

The river ahead was a swift flowing, muddy torrent forty feet wide and four feet deep. Alou and Frederico didn't slow down through the undulating rapids as they held Paha aloft above their shoulders. Alou was in front holding up her father's head and shoulders and Frederico in back struggling to keep his own head and Paha's broken leg out of the churning water.

A life of hard work had made Alou strong. She would

need all her strength today. Her father had lost large amounts of weight since his injury and internal bruising kept him from eating. This had reduced him to a sack of broken bones and skin weighing less then 100 pounds.

"Keep his head up! We can do it!" Alou kept calling out. She was way past her second wind and into the adrenaline gripped flow of the supernatural.

For a second Paha lost his rolled tule mat in the water. With lightening speed he thrust his good arm into the river and grabbed his sacred satchel. Frederico was struck by Paha's determination. He still had incredible focus and was very much in control of his profound destiny.

On and on they ventured. To make it around the first rocky point Alou attached a fiber strap under the armpits of Paha and made a headband out of the other end. This enabled her to completely support Paha on her back and shoulders as she climbed across the thin rocky shelf. Frederico helped Alou the best his short cramping body could. Together they could triumph over the limitations of the human form. Every time they slowed Paha would sing his power song to the spirits and electrifying charges of energy would rejuvenate all of them.

Alou's sheer determination to help her father, in Frederico's mind, was the ultimate sign of love and respect. It was uplifting emotionally and he wanted to be a part of that. Her dedication became his and the boy's strength of spirit became Alou's as well.

Alou's fatherly love motivated Frederico to find the love within his heart for his father. The Captain had changed. The whole sad saga with Paha had awakened his interest in getting to know Frederico. His newfound respect and admiration for his son became an iron bond that couldn't be broken. Frederico ached for a reunification with his father. For the first time the boy saw the extreme importance of his father's love. The example that Alou had recently set showed Alou's heart was in the right place and Frederico vowed to follow her example.

Darkness approached on the shortest day of the year. There wasn't much time left before the sun went down so Alou picked up the pace, leaving the game and determined Frederico gasping for air.

One last treacherous stretch remained before they arrived at the winter solstice cave. Their pace stalled when Paha convulsed with pain at the base of a large cliff. Alou laid him down on the trail and pleaded with him to stay in this world.

"Paha, my father, our love will never die. I'll help you Paha. I'm here for you and will always be," she whispered to her critically injured father.

He whispered something into Alou's ear and pointed up at the shear face of the cliff. Overlooking the vast white-capped steel gray ocean, up more then one hundred feet, lay the carefully disguised opening to Paha's secret winter solstice cave. Alou looked up and said something to her father.

He shook his head yes, confirming the cave's existence. There was one other very important thing he told her. Only Frederico could help him the rest of the way. She must stay below at the base of the cliff and wait.

Up until now she had not known of the cave's exact location. When she realized how difficult it was going to be she started to cry. She was terrified of failing Paha after trying so hard to get him there in time.

Paha sat up and touched her face. His gentle, fatherly

caress soothed her fears and stopped her tears. The old native pulled her face close and embraced her, patiently patting the sorrows away. After a long minute he looked into her eyes and smiled wide, playfully giving her a little wink. She laughed softly, took a big deep breath and exhaled slowly in a long sigh. Alou said,

"Frederico, my father's ready. It's time to climb but this is where I must stop. Only you and my father can venture into the winter solstice cave but you must hurry. Darkness approaches."

"Alou, I'm not sure I can carry him up there. Please help me. You're strong. With you he'll make it. With me, we might fail!" Frederico confided, unsure of his limits.

"No Frederico, I can't go. You have the inner strength and your spirit will see to it that you use all of it," she said with power and pride.

"Why? Alou tell me, what does he need to do. I don't know about such things. Tell me what I can do!" Frederico cried.

"Our survival depends on this Frederico. The sun god has been dropping steadily on the horizon every day. Without the winter solstice ceremony the sun will sink so low we will never see the bright of day again. My father, as shaman, must ensure the sun comes back. In our winter solstice ceremony he will pull the sun back with his sun staff. I'm sure you saw him with it before we left. It's in his tule satchel. Only Paha knows the right words to say. Trust me, this is of the utmost importance."

Alou's big brown eyes cut through the apprehension and filled Frederico with determination and confidence.

Paha started singing a new song, far higher in pitch and intensity.

"You must go now!" Alou ordered, keenly aware of the essence of time.

Alou helped Paha to his feet and Frederico came up and supported him under his one good arm. With the fading light the rancho boy and the old native man felt their way up the cliff using natural fissures and cracks to cling to. The native man never quit despite his obvious agony. He was an inspiration to Frederico.

Paha's memory served him well as he avoided dead end routes up the cliff face. Surprisingly, Frederico's strength grew in leaps and bounds as they came closer to the cave. Paha sang faintly the whole time. Clear low notes that kept the spring in his legs and hope in his heart. As long as he could sing Paha was strong.

It was pitch black out by the time they reached the mouth of the cave. Paha felt his way into the eroded opening and called out loudly to announce his presence. The sound echoed through the long deep chamber, moving Paha to laughter, a sprightly happy laugh full of renewal.

Frederico kept silent and huddled next to his friend in a depression on the floor of the cave. Soft sand filled the pit and their combined body heat kept them warm.

All during the night Paha continued to chant and sing to the spirits. When his pain became unbearable Frederico would comfort the man, talking to him, encouraging him in Spanish, praising him for his powerful spirit.

This helped to motivate Paha and sustained him. His low songs were slow moans now. Paha's life was fading but Frederico's spirit grew stronger.

"Please Paha, you must hold on. Only a bit longer!" Frederico begged.

The boy could see the beginning of light behind the

distant mountains and knew it was only a matter of minutes before winter solstice arrived.

Paha pointed at his tule satchel and urged the boy to bring it to him. Frederico took it over, untied it, and opened it across the cave floor. The faint light from the coming day illuminated the cave just enough to reveal cave walls completely covered in sacred art. Everywhere there were symbols of the sun, pinwheels with ticks, incredibly colorful rock paintings of all sizes and shapes.

In the middle of the cave floor there was a shallow stick hole that had been pecked into the sandstone. With mere seconds remaining before solstice Paha crawled over to the hole with his sun staff and placed the butt end into the socket. Paha tried to pull himself to his knees but didn't have the strength so Frederico rushed over and lifted him, helping him up to the proper position. Paha kept watching the distant mountain range, waiting for the absolute critical second. Sensing it was near Paha launched into a beautiful, high-spirited song, swaying from side to side. The movements brought visions of life and the everlasting spirit within.

As the first rays of the sun streaked over the ridge line Paha uttered some strong native words and pulled the sun staff back in a long slow deliberate stroke. At that instant, the spirit of the boy and the man became one and an indescribable energy flooded the cave.

Paha fell backwards and collapsed onto the floor, landing on his tule mat and soft sand. Frederico watched as the color faded from his native friend's face leaving him bone white. The boy knew Paha was passing to the spirit world. He felt proud to be a part of this and honored to usher his spirit to the great beyond.

Frederico bent over and touched Paha on the head,

yearning to feel his last living breath. His touch sparked Paha to life for one last moment. Paha opened his eyes and looked into the spirit of joy and rebirth. At that instant Frederico was drenched in the new light of day. The boy drew near and Paha whispered very slowly and deliberately in Spanish,

"Frederico, my friend" and smiled with that special gleam in his eyes as his spirit passed quietly into the new light to soar with the eagles for the rest of eternity.

Frederico felt an incredible sense of relief and reverence for this special man. Paha lived his life the way he saw fit, true to his native ways until the very end. Out of honor for Frederico he spoke the boy's Spanish language for the first time. Frederico knew this was significant and was overcome by its profound implications.

Frederico felt his own heart, the beat strong and steady, his life changed forever by Paha. He vowed to live his life in honor of him. To use his knowledge, his brief glimpse of native ways, to glorify those who came first.

Frederico peered down the cliff to where Alou waited and climbed down to embrace her.

"Paha is gone," Frederico said,

"But a new day dawns and life is renewed," the boy added, smiling wide.

Alou, the wonderful mother, devoted daughter, and proud native gave the boy an extra hard squeeze and wiped away her own tears of joy. Alou sang a special song to her father, her final goodbye echoing against the cliffs.

They walked back to the river mouth where the Captain was waiting. A caring witness to the whole transcending episode, Frederico's devotion to Paha had touched the Captain's heart. There was much to be gained by becoming a part of his son's life and he intended on finding out the happy truth.

Paha's passing helped mold Frederico into a fine man of integrity and responsibility. In the ensuing weeks, with newfound courage, Frederico confronted Miguel and persuaded him to change his abusive ways. Brimming with confidence Frederico approached his father and opened discussions on how to rethink his native prejudices. To accept the natives for who they really were, vital members of the symphony of life.

THE END